MYTHBUSTERS

The Explosive Truth Behind 30 of the Most Perplexing Urban Legends of All Time

by KEITH and KENT ZIMMERMAN

with Jamie Hyneman, Adam Savage, and Peter Rees

SIMON SPOTLIGHT ENTERTAINMENT
New York London Toronto Sydney

SIMON SPOTLIGHT ENTERTAINMENT
An imprint of Simon & Schuster
1230 Avenue of the Americas, New York, New York 10020

Manufactured in the United States of America

10 9

Library of Congress Control Number 2005926821
ISBN-13: 978-1-4169-0929-3
ISBN-10: 1-4169-0929-X

THE *MYTHBUSTERS* BOOK DEVELOPMENT TEAM:
Peter Rees, Executive Producer, Beyond Productions
Jane Root, General Manager, Discovery Channel
Gena McCarthy, Executive Producer, Discovery Channel
Sharon M. Bennett, Senior Vice President, Strategic Partnerships & Licensing
Michael Malone, Vice President, Licensing
Carol LeBlanc, Vice President, Marketing & Retail Development
Elizabeth Bakacs, Creative Director, Strategic Partnerships
Erica Jacobs Green, Director of Publishing
Elsa Abraham, Publishing Manager
Erica Rose, Publishing Associate

Acknowledgments

The Z'men wish to thank: Adam, Jamie, and Peter, and the whole *MythBusters* crew; Erica Rose, Erica Green, and Elsa Abraham at Discovery; Ryan Fischer-Harbage and Beth Bracken at SSE; Arielle Eckstut; and a shout-out to our brothers at H-Unit.

Contents

Killer Robots, Chicken Guns, and Blueprints: A Week in the Life of MythBusters

From the outside, Jamie Hyneman's workshop may seem like just another workshop in San Francisco's south side industrial district, where the streets are named after different states of the Union. But from the inside, it is a wonderland, home to Hyneman's visual effects shop. It's a fascinating space— two floors of walls covered with hanging props and movie posters. Robots and creepy rubbery critters and fake food line the shelves. These days it's a full-time battle for Jamie, who has a highly regimented sense of order and control, to keep the place tidy. He's always turning off lights, picking up trash, sweeping up, cleaning up the kitchen and bathroom, and trying to keep the shop neat now that his business has been paired with *MythBusters*, Discovery Channel's hit science-fact television series, which he cohosts. Only recently, since the aquisition of more studios and ancillary offices only a mile or so down the road, has Jamie gotten a little relief.

Adam and Jamie have a great relationship, but Jamie jokes, "Adam is extremely aggravating to work with because he's destructive with my tools. He's erratic, but I embrace that difference. We both do."

"You should see Jamie's house," cracks *MythBusters* cohost Adam Savage. "It looks like he just moved in. There's nothing inside it."

Down the hall from Jamie's clean office (on whose tabletop they used to shoot the early blueprint drawings), Adam and the show's rambunctious creator, Peter Rees, share cluttered quarters. Their work area is certainly nothing fancy. Both Adam and Peter work amid stacks of papers and assorted DVD-ROMs and various mechanical gewgaws. At least Adam has a desk. Rees, a rugged Australian documentary director and producer, works behind a folding table. A few folding chairs are available for spontaneous production meetings.

In an adjoining room are more desks for the research staff. The researcher uses the phone for things like trying to track down a swimming pool that the MythBusters can fire live ammunition into (more on that later), while the wall behind him is a scheduling board with dozens and dozens of slips of paper representing bust-able myths past, present, future, and absolutely out of the question. It's not uncommon to see Rees pounding away at his laptop computer, plotting new ideas or sending off scores of e-mail replies. Adam might be outside, excited about his car (at least while it was brand-new)—not a Benz or a Jag, but a retro-cool Mini Cooper. Inside, Jamie often gives a tour of his facilities: the hallowed sanctuary, the famed laboratory where the MythBusters triumph and fail their way through modern mythology and scientific experimentation. Jamie beams with a pride of ownership while explaining the inner workings of a few football linebacker–sized robots. Around the corner Buster, the world's most famous and abused crash test dummy, lies on his back, conked out lifelessly on an ambulance gurney.

Rees is the third MythBuster, or maybe even the first, since the show was his original creation and carries his indelible stamp of twisted scientific innovation. *MythBusters* may have been his brainchild, and he is the closest thing to a director the show has, but he's far from

possessive, giving his celebrated cohosts tremendous creative license while at the same time providing firm direction and feedback in return. It's Rees who goes to the mat while attempting to serve two scientists/inventors and laboring with Discovery Channel and Beyond Productions, a major television and movie production house that is headquartered in Sydney. He's a producer, director, scientific consultant, and floor manager all rolled into one.

"I'd been making science documentaries for Discovery for a decade," says Rees. In fact, he's incredibly educated, with postgraduate degrees in film and environmental management and an undergraduate degree in archaeology.

"Peter can manage any environment except this one," jokes Adam.

After collecting his bouquet of degrees, Rees graduated from the Australian Film, Television, and Radio School, the leading government-funded film school Down Under.

"I love science and irrelevant stuff. I've done documentaries on things like the assassin caterpillar."

When he wasn't filming fire ants, platypuses, and brown recluse spiders, Peter Rees was making frequent trips to America, filming documentaries for the noted Australian science show *Beyond 2000*. One was on gladiator robot wars, which was where he ran into one Jamie Hyneman and his friend and employee Adam Savage. The pair had wreaked havoc in the robot world with Blendo the Killer Automaton. When it came time years later to locate a host for a brand-new irreverent science show he was pitching to Discovery Channel, one of the first people to pop into Rees's head was the mustached, laconic Hyneman.

"Back in Australia," says Rees, "when this idea came up, we knew we wanted someone who could build anything. Someone who had their own shop, because we didn't want a studio. We wanted the show to be rough as guts. We needed someone who had all the tools. The final criterion was someone who might be interesting on television."

Originally, *MythBusters* was going to feature a builder and an investigator.

After sifting through several audition reels, it was Jamie and Adam who first caught the eye of Beyond and, ultimately, Discovery. When they finally decided on the special effects pair, Peter and Beyond got a little bit of both in their cohosts, and a lot more technical know-how and camera presence than they'd originally bargained for.

"Discovery instantly loved them," says Rees. "They were exactly the kind of guys they expected we'd get. In fact, their exact comment was, 'This is just what we need, a couple of eggheads from San Francisco.'"

According to Rees, Discovery instantly requested three programs, which became the original *MythBusters* pilots. It appears as though Discovery knew the show was going to be a hit before Peter had even made the first three programs.

After Jamie and Adam were locked in, Rees came over with a small crew and shot those first episodes in five weeks.

"We planned on doing three stories per episode. We had a fantastic time. The three of us hit it off straightaway. They *could* build anything. They knew what they were doing. We had a laugh."

It's midweek and Peter and the MythBusters are in the midst of filming a couple of experiments, both at different stages. In their studio, Adam and Jamie are seated at the "blueprint table," where the pair shoots the introduction and lead-ins to whatever myths they're tackling next. The studio is a virtual *MythBusters* museum. Fans of the show would recognize every piece crammed on the shelves and all of the props surrounding the table.

Hanging from the ceiling is the triangular raft in which Jamie and Adam escaped from Alcatraz. There's also a wooden box of broken plate glass sheets from the Chicken Gun Revisited experiment. Across the room is the chicken gun itself, minus its long barrel, which was later co-opted for the Scuba Diver Forest Fire myth. Both Needle-in-the-Haystack contraptions live inside the studio. Also overhead is Jamie's yellow surfboard hovercraft.

It's from the studio's table that Jamie and Adam describe to the camera the latest myth in production. The show is unscripted, so it requires a couple of quick run-throughs before the three settle on a final take. Peter sits at the table as well, as always carefully off-camera, coaching the guys through the scientific intricacies. Jamie and Adam are quick learners. In only a couple of run-throughs, the take is nailed. After finishing the intros and the jovial and sardonic exchanges, Adam is elected to scribble and draw on the blueprint as a cameraman hovers over his shoulder. Then it's back over to the other *MythBusters* studio to tend to a more serious matter—the next experiment.

At the main studio, the other experiment is in hotter, heavier, and more uncertain territory. Peter and the MythBusters are testing yet another Hollywood-fueled myth: You can survive being shot at by diving into water. Just the day before shooting, Jamie and Adam built an oblong chamber of horrors: a 12-inch-square and nearly 12-foot-high steel and Plexiglas tower. The inch-thick Plexiglas sides had previously been Jamie's display shelves, holding a decade's worth of his model creatures in the foyer of the studio. In order for Jamie and Adam to survey the structure for leaks, it was filled with water.

The idea is for Jamie to fire a frightening succession of firearms into the tower of water to see how fast (or slowly) a bullet passes through water and into a foot-square block of ballistics gel floating in the tank. (Clearly the mucus-colored gel is the duct tape of the MythBusters—they use it for everything.)

As Peter eggs him on, Jamie rides the scissor lift to the top of the tank in order to shoot a 9mm round straight into the water. Cameras have been rigged from the ceiling, from the sides of the tank, and even in the water. This is a test, not only of the tank's ability to hold water, but to see what slow-motion camera shots Peter can expect to incorporate into the story. After everyone has donned proper ear and eye protection, Jamie counts off and fires a round that drops feebly into the tank, only to run out of steam after about 8 feet of water before it gently plunks down onto the block of gel. Adam and Peter are excited—the test result means that during the official filming, they will probably be able to shoot the full-range arsenal they have lined up, after all. The plan is to blast the tank with weapons in the following order: a BB gun, a 9mm pistol, a shotgun with a deer slug, a black powder rifle with a homemade lead slug, a standard M1 rifle, and finally, the mother of all firearms, a Second Amendment–protected Ramboesque .50-caliber rifle, the same firearm used as a defensive weapon against tanks.

Jamie is skeptical, especially about firing a .50-caliber bullet (nicknamed "banana") inside his workshop. A few firearm experts have already warned the researcher that the shot could blow out his shop's windows, collapse the water tank, drill through both 1-inch planks of Plexiglas at the bottom of the tower tank *and* into Jamie's concrete floor, and cause permanent hearing loss to those in the room.

Peter, undeterred and ever the instigator, plows ahead to get the biggest burst. Adam is so sure that 10 feet of water will stop all the bullets that he offers up $100 bets. But Adam's enthusiasm is contagious. No takers.

Two days later the experiment is ready to be filmed. The guns are rolled in, including the 9mm pistol, a 12-gauge shotgun with its solid 1-ounce deer slug, an 1853 Enfield muzzle-loading rifle, an M1 World War II standard-issue rifle, and finally, the big kahuna, the .50 caliber.

"Does it come in pink?" Jamie asks, as the jet-black .50 caliber is carted into the workshop, ominously housed in a wooden coffinlike case.

The cameras are ready to roll. Jamie takes his place at the top of the tank to fire the 9mm at a 90-degree angle into the water, the worst-case scenario if you are being shot at while underwater. The shot is fired. The round used this time produces a more aggressive reaction and makes it through the block of gel near the bottom of the tank.

Next, Jamie gets set to fire the shotgun. After the countdown, he pulls the trigger—but that wasn't all. With that, a tremendous geyser of water sprays him, the force of the blast ruptures the tank, and a hundred gallons of water gush all over Jamie's floor. The remainder of the afternoon is spent mopping and cleaning up Jamie's workshop. No divas. Everybody pitches in.

The experiment is halted. For the moment.

The thought of firing the .50-caliber stop-a-tank gun is now a joke. But within the hour, the researcher has a line on a municipal swimming pool in South San Francisco that has been tagged for renovation. Seems the city workers are big fans of the show. Still, the myth is looking very shaky. Plus, it's looking doubtful that Peter will be able to get his .50-caliber bang.

"This is the most difficult show that Beyond has ever produced," says Rees, sitting in Jamie's office. "By its nature, everything is experimental. We really don't know what's going to happen." Rees, as producer, deals with multiple concerns, especially safety. But when all safety precautions are in place and the cameras roll, the reaction is rewarding.

"We have people telling us that we've just inspired the next generation of scientists," Peter says, beaming. "What more can we ask for?"

A big issue, however, more so with Jamie and Peter than with Adam, is the reputation the show is gaining for "blowing things up."

"We get approached by the public all the time," says Jamie, "in the grocery store or someplace. Some guy will look at me and say, 'Blow something up!' But that's only one end of the spectrum here. The other end is that we gather an audience because we blow stuff up—teenagers, school kids of all ages, adults—and because we eventually suck people in who like to follow the process. Before they know it, they're enjoying something that's thought-provoking."

TWELVE MYTHS YOU'LL PROBABLY NEVER SEE BROKEN ON *MYTHBUSTERS*

Here are a dozen myths on the production bulletin board that for one reason or another were deemed unacceptable to be tried by the MythBusters.

1. Paper Crossbow: A prison inmate builds a fatal crossbow out of paper, the elastic in his underpants, and a sharpened tip from a food tray.

2. 21 Grams: When you die, as your soul leaves your body, do you lose 21 grams?

3. Airplanes and Cell Phones: Does using a cell phone aboard an airliner really endanger the safety of the other passengers?

4. Do alligators really grow in the sewer?

5. Twinkie Defense: Does eating too much junk food affect your judgment and behavior?

6. Flat VW: Is it possible that a flattened VW bug was found in between a head-on collision of two massive semi trucks?

7. Birds in Truck: Can a truckload of 1,000 pigeons cause a truck to levitate if it hits a bump?

8. Card Cannon: Is it possible to create an explosive weapon by scraping the surface of a playing card?

9. Chinese Junk: In 1421, did a Chinese junk make it all the way to the west coast of the United States and sail the delta region of Sacramento?

10. Nintendo v. Professional: Are video games breeding the fighter pilots of tomorrow?

11. Hybrid Car Rescue: Are firefighters and rescue teams hesitant to rescue drivers trapped inside hybrid cars with the "jaws of life" because of fear of electrocution?

12. Stars from a Well: If you dig a deep enough hole with a small enough arc of visible sky, can you see the stars during the day?

Peter agrees. "We hate it when people ask us to blow stuff up. We're not interested in blowing stuff up. I mean, we do it, but it's not what we primarily do. Most science programs preach to the converted. They're designed for an audience that's receptive to science, while we're trying to convert the preachers, if that's possible."

Still, the MythBusters owe much of their success to their ability to balance science with entertainment, which sometimes involves . . . well, blowing stuff up.

From the beginning, *MythBusters* has had a one-sentence credo that every crew member now wears on the back of their T-shirts: "We don't just retell the legends, we put them to the test." Other *MythBusters* T-shirt truisms include "Human Guinea Pigs" and "I Am My Own Stunt Double."

"Our philosophy," cites Rees, "is that we try to replicate the circumstances of the myth, and if that fails, we try to replicate the results and outcome of the myth. Every single story is structured that way.

"The criteria for busting a myth," he continues, "are three grades: Busted, Plausible, and Confirmed. 'Busted' is a situation in which we can't reproduce the outcome and there is no documentation of any kind that supports the mythical outcome. 'Plausible' is the middle ground where we can, in some instances, replicate the results, but there is no documentation that shows that it ever happened. Or there is documentation, but we can't reproduce it. We have to go to some extra length. 'Confirmed' is when we have documentation and we were able to reproduce it."

The current myth in question is: "You can survive being shot at by diving into water." Busted, plausible, or confirmed?

Early the next week, the swimming pool has been lined up. Cutting the original tower tank in half, Adam has constructed a rig filled with blocks of ballistics gel that, once placed in the pool, will serve to catch bullets. The rig is put into the water. An extra ballistics screen is added in the unlikely event that

Jamie's shots are errant. The show is back on the road and the moment of truth has arrived.

Will the myth be busted, confirmed, or worse, deemed plausible? Will the MythBusters crew be able to run the gamut of their arsenal, shooting a series of noisy rounds from a cacophony of weaponry, from the BB gun to the granddaddy .50 caliber? Will Peter get his dream shot of Adam at the bottom of the pool, dodging bullets? Will the insurers allow such a foolhardy venture? Most important, will the MythBusters prove once and for all whether you can survive being shot at by simply diving into water? And if so, how much water and how deep? Will yet another Hollywood myth bite the bullet?

To find out the answers, tune in to *MythBusters,* where another myth is once again tested the hard way, all in a day's work for a MythBuster. Oh yeah, and don't try it at home.

Adam Savage: Speed Building and the Vertical Learning Curve

Who *are* the MythBusters? In terms of personality and temperament, Adam Savage and Jamie Hyneman in real life are as worlds apart as they are on the show. Adam is playful, animated, and impulsive; Jamie is earnest, contemplative, and methodical. Adam rides around inside the *MythBuster* shop on a motorbike; Jamie patches up the holes in the walls and repairs the gouges in the floor. Adam is the conversationalist, while Jamie is much more reserved.

These guys are different, all right. They're also easily identifiable on the street. Adam is known for dressing in the familiar black leather coat and tan fedora "costume" he's worn for the past five years; while Jamie, with his trademark walrus 'stache and his crisp white shirts, is unmistakable. The duo is like a special effects Laurel and Hardy; together they could be aptly described as characters and caricatures.

"I can disguise myself easily with different clothes," Adam says. "Whereas I *might be* 'that guy' on television, Jamie *is* 'that guy.' When I go out with him, we get recognized a lot more."

The MythBusters are truly recognizable as two guys with diametrically opposed temperaments. But they also share some very important traits. Both possess an intense work ethic. Both prefer to build stuff at lightning speed, using an education process that Adam laughingly refers to as "the vertical learning curve."

"While there are great differences in our methodologies and in the way we perceive and use intuition," Adam concedes, "the one thing that both of us respect about the other, which neither of us has ever found in another person, is if you give either one of us an assignment to build—from a space suit to a needle-in-a-haystack finder—we'll finish it by the end of the day."

Fans of *MythBusters* know that Adam and Jamie have more than three decades of special effects experience. But what's not so well known are some of the specific projects Adam Savage worked on behind the scenes before becoming a well-known MythBuster. If you're the kind of person who stays until the very last name rolls off the credits at the movies, you might already know that Adam spent years working primarily as a model maker on such high-profile film projects as the *Matrix* films, *Terminator 3*, and *Star Wars*. Building models for movies

and commercials was where Adam and Jamie first crossed paths on the West Coast. But prior to moving to the West Coast during the late eighties, Adam Savage spent his formative years growing up in New York City.

To say that Adam Savage came from an artistic family would be putting it mildly. Adam's father, W. Lee Savage, was a master painter and eccentric individual. According to Adam's sister, Kate Savage-Friedman, Lee Savage "was a realist painter who worked in acrylic paint and later etching, often with a surrealist or psychological twist. His subject matters included landscapes, still life, complex multifigure genre painting and many, many portraits." In 1962 PBS shot a documentary entitled *Four American Artists*. The four painters featured were Andy Warhol, Roy Lichtenstein, Robert Motherwell, and Adam's father, Lee Savage.

"He was an amazing painter who avoided fame at all costs," Kate said of her father. "But his first one-man show in New York in 1959 sold out to the Whitneys and the Hirschhorns. They bought all of the paintings out of the show. At that point, he was doing so well, everything he painted was sold. Then he began painting imitations of his own work because it was so lucrative. Then he stopped showing completely and applied for a Guggenheim. On his grant application, under the reason why he painted, he wrote only, 'I paint for the same reason I splash in the bathtub.' He got the grant and went off to England to paint for a few more years."

Adam grew up with television in his blood. During the golden age of television, his father provided for the Savage family by working as a noted television director for his own successful and influential production agency, Savage Friedman. He directed classic commercial campaigns for big brand-name consumer products. But he stopped suddenly.

"My father got out because he eventually found it soul crushing. So he raised my sister and me while doing animated spots for *Sesame Street*. I was a member of the Screen Actors Guild by the time I was seven. I did voiceovers for him back then," Adam says.

By the time Adam was fourteen, the acting bug bit, and he aced his first audition as a young grocery clerk in a Charmin toilet tissue ad, opposite Mr. Whipple. As a public school student, Adam was a coaster. He got through high school with a solid B average (though he was capable of achieving much more). Then after high school, it was off to New York University's acting program.

"There was always a ton of support at home to do the creative thing. I want to learn things at my pace. I'm an absorber of information. I like to collect skills. Knowing just enough about a skill to know when you can use it and when you can apply it to solve a problem, that's the critical factor."

After leaving NYU, Adam knocked around Manhattan working at graphic design and sculpting, eking out a living from a series of jobs while showing his work in local art galleries. "Every job I've ever had, I've had for either a year or an hour. No in between for me. If the people I worked for were jerks or if the job wasn't rewarding, I might go out for a soda and never come back," he admits. Through it all, he had a hankering to break into special effects. In addition, young Adam developed a keen interest in circus art and taught himself how to expertly juggle, throw high-speed playing cards, and unicycle inside the fountain at Washington Square.

In 1989 he found himself in San Francisco (where *MythBusters* tapes its shows), leaving behind a cooperative art gallery on New York's Lower East Side. Adam was immediately smitten by the City by the Bay. "When I first visited in 1987 I thought it was the most beautiful city I'd ever seen, and I was only standing on the corner of Gough and Lombard. So I knew I was in for a treat," he remembered.

Armed with a healthy shot of optimism, Adam cracked into the art and special effects scene in the Bay Area. He scored a job at a performance space doing carpentry, building riggings, doing technical direction, and running the crew.

Adam's reputation grew steadily on the theater circuit as his art and set designs became more and more unusual. While he built a remote control La-Z-Boy recliner for another theater rep group across the Bay, several of his theater friends were getting calls from Jamie Hyneman to come work on a commercial for Nabisco. Jamie had just taken over an ailing portion of a San Francisco special effects house that eventually became his own M5 Industries. It was there that Jamie began to hear about "this guy Adam" through the other designers. Adam soon got the call from Jamie and showed up for his interview with a suitcase full of what he referred to as "cool stuff I'd built." Within a week he was hired, and Adam spent four years as one of Jamie's head model makers, working on a hundred television commercials, a handful of feature films, and assorted music videos.

"I got a reputation for being able to build props quickly," admits Adam.

After very productive years with Jamie and a short stint at a start-up toy company, Adam eventually found himself where he'd always dreamed he'd end up, at the legendary Industrial Light and Magic, George Lucas's famed production and effects house in Marin County.

During Adam's first day at ILM, while his friends labored on *Star Wars: Episode I,* he was assigned to a bank commercial. First assignment: build a painfully exact half-scale model of a banker's desk in two weeks (a luxurious amount of time for Adam). "I built the perfect banker's desk, right down to the perfect wood grain on the desktop," he says.

For another project, he built a miniature bathroom. "Every nut, bolt, washer, and gasket had to be accurate to the original. Because the camera was so close in, it had to look full scale, right down to the thousands of tiles. Yet what you see filling the screen is only twelve inches wide."

The life of a model builder, set designer, and special-effects man was a wildly unpredictable one, but Adam rode it out and enjoyed his time at ILM.

It was while working with ILM that Adam heard from his former boss Jamie Hyneman regarding a strange television proposal called *MythBusters.*

"Jamie called me in February of 2002. He'd just gotten a call from Peter Rees," Adam remembers. The three had met back in 1996, when Rees interviewed Adam and Jamie as part of a documentary he was shooting. Jamie told Adam that Rees, a daredevil Aussie cowboy documentary filmmaker with an inordinate interest in science and modern mythology, had an unusual idea.

"They're thinking of doing a show called *MythBusters*," Jamie said.

Rees's call solicited Jamie as a possible host for the show. It was Jamie who immediately mentioned Adam's name to Rees. Together, Jamie figured, the two could work nicely and in tandem as an out-of-the-ordinary, on-camera team.

And so, for *MythBusters*, Adam and Jamie resumed their partnership building stuff. A slim crew, comprising Jamie, Peter, Adam, and a location scout, shot a series of MythBusting experiments that would later be molded into the three one-hour pilot episodes. After a decade of walking the art and special effects high wire, Adam finally saw his life, as hectic as it had become, fall into place. Now, despite their differences, Adam and Jamie share a respectful and productive working relationship.

Adam admits, "My failing is that I tend to be too elaborate sometimes. One of the great things that Jamie brings to the table is the main question, 'What is the root of what we're trying to do?' Most times he's right, as the simple, elegant solution he often brings is a terrific boon toward getting things done on time."

With their intense work ethic, practical resourcefulness, and depth of skills, it's hard to imagine another set of hosts more capable of handling the impossible MythBusting deadlines than Adam and Jamie, who do it week in and week out.

Adam explains, "Jamie and I are most at odds about central approaches. I like to have things happen superfast. I like to eliminate time constraints whenever I can. If you give me a choice to fill up a tank in three hours for zero money and almost no effort versus fill it up in fifteen minutes with a bunch of phone calls and some fire hose, I'm going to choose the fifteen minutes because that leaves more time to take care of other problems.

"That said, there are a ton of solutions I come up with by asking myself, 'What would Jamie do? What's the Jamie solution?' Peter's biggest challenge early on was slowing us down and getting us to stop and understand why we were doing what we were doing. There was a lot of back and forth that first year between Jamie, Peter, and myself. I'll go through a set of parameters in my head incredibly fast. When I do that I'll fall or break something because I'm moving too fast."

Adam Savage, the fastest MythBuster and master blaster builder in the West?

"One thing about learning skills real fast: You can go to school for welding and mechanical design, but there's no school you can go to that will teach you how to make donuts out of foam rubber. I can screw up, start again from scratch, and still be faster than someone who is overthinking the problem. That's the goal."

Jamie Hyneman: Animatronics, Robots, and *MythBusters*

O n camera, Jamie Hyneman is perceived as the cool, monotoned, supreme builder of all things. Off camera, he is fluent in Russian and able to read several languages, including Spanish, French, and several other Slavic languages. Of the MythBusters' thirty total years of experience in movie special effects, nearly twenty of those belong to Jamie, the man who wears the black beret, the crisp white shirts, and a trademark walrus mustache.

It was while living in New York City in the 1980s that Jamie first delved into what the movie industry calls "animatronics," a buzzword generally referring to complicated mechanical puppetry powered by motors and servos. Animatronics typically involves radio controls, complicated linkages, and microcircuitry, of which Jamie is a master. Because he was inherently handy with a table saw and welding torch, Jamie was first hired to help oversee the model shop of a New York production house, where one of his early jobs was to build 8-foot-tall hallucinogenic Potatoheads for a Cheech and Chong film.

By 1990 Jamie and his wife had relocated to San Francisco, where he pursued the animatronics trade even more aggressively. Although Los Angeles was the Mecca for model building and special effects work, the lure of San Francisco during the post–*Star Wars* era prevailed. Upon arriving in the Bay

Area, Jamie was hired at a large effects house. There he worked on major Hollywood motion pictures like *Arachnophobia* (he designed the creepy spiders) and *RoboCop*. In addition, he worked on animation for hundreds of commercials. If it involved dancing food, jiggy cereal morsels, robotic soft drink machines, or animation clips, chances were good that Jamie might be behind the scenes, making the impossible seem real with stop-motion animation.

"When I went to work for the effects house," says Jamie, "my first job was for a cleaning fluid commercial. We had to select thirty pine trees that were as large as we could find, fifteen to twenty feet tall. We put them on a stage, and I had to rig these little rolling carts with levers, using two-by-fours and bungee cords, to make the pines look like this walking forest. I remember we had sixty people pumping on these levers, pushing these trees with their branches waving back and forth.

"I logged in several commercials, one after the other. Sometimes it was a cheese commercial, where you're wiggling a piece of cheese in front of the camera. Other times it got quite involved, building water tanks for splash effects, working with film crews, directors, producers, clients, and TV celebrities. I was very hands-on, very active."

Jamie is often pegged as the less whimsical, more urbane and methodical MythBuster, but in his other life as a special effects technician, he often has to come up with strange ideas to please film directors, like the time he poured 300 gallons of milk into a pool for a chocolate company commercial.

While furthering his reputation as a builder, Jamie spent part of the 1990s dabbling in "CG," computer graphics, knowing that computer graphics might eventually overtake animatronics as the main purveyor of cinematic special effects. Although both technologies coexist on the screen today, Jamie much prefers the brawn and ingenuity of animatronics to spending hours in front of a computer screen creating computerized graphics and special effects.

"Yes, you are working in the movies. But in reality you're sitting at a desk," Jamie says. Just sitting at a desk has never been something Jamie Hyneman enjoyed.

A major turning point in Jamie's special effects career involved the creation of a killer robot named Blendo. In 1990 the sport of designing and building gladiator robots became the high-tech rage. When Jamie first heard about the live contest known as *Robot Wars,* he jumped at the chance to compete. But rather than enter a typical robot on wheels with armlike and leglike appendages, he designed a carnivorous automaton. The robot was essentially a domed monster whose main piece of armor was an inverted Chinese wok, and whose weapons were two lawnmower blades rotating dangerously at 70 miles per hour (mph).

Blendo was Jamie's answer to the question, "What if you made something that spun really fast, so fast that you wouldn't even need a motor on it? You'd get it going like a top and it would take so long to wind down that by the time you were done with the match, anything Blendo touched would be instantly destroyed."

And that's exactly what happened. Every time Blendo entered the *Robot Wars* arena, it made metallic mincemeat out of its opponents in seconds. Blendo was a vicious competitor, and the *Robot Wars* organizers gave Jamie and his team the trophy and first prize money. Blendo returned the following year and would later play an even more important part in Jamie's professional career.

"The next year," Jamie recalls, "within seconds of the second match, we ripped the whole face off our opponent. Nuts and bolts flew everywhere, but Blendo was intact. When we showed up with Blendo the whole pit area would get silent and I'd be off to the side with a file, sharpening my blades and grinning."

Jamie and his team held the heavyweight title for the *Robot Wars* combat competition for two consecutive years. It was during that time that Australian documentary filmmaker Peter Rees shot a piece on the spectator sport, interviewing Jamie and his pit crew, which also included another animatronics technician named Adam Savage.

Soon enough, another opportunity came about for Jamie. Due to the declining fortunes in San Francisco's movie industry, the effects company he worked for was downsizing. Just before going under, they sold Hyneman their model shop facilities for one dollar. Years later the shop would become home for Rees's new show, a peculiar science show called *MythBusters*.

Jamie Hyneman was born and raised on a farm in Columbus, Indiana. Jamie was working in the apple orchards before graduating from high school, when his father convinced him to buy the local pet store. In addition to selling gerbils, birds, and dog food, over the three years Jamie operated the pet store he purchased various snakes and even raised a lion cub, which grew up guarding and prowling the Hyneman farm.

After Jamie became bored with the pet store, he decided to sell the business and attend college. Though he was originally an art major with an emphasis on sculpture, Jamie changed course and four years later earned a degree in Russian linguistics from Indiana University, with minors in French and Japanese. As part of his language requirements, Jamie became fluent in Russian and French. While living in the Midwest, Jamie worked summers as a concrete inspector and an Italian cook. Halfway through working on a master's degree in library science, he decided to vacation in the  Caribbean. Not content to merely lounge on the beach, he took sailing lessons and dreamed of becoming a crew member on a charter boat. The vacation became extended.

"I went to St. Thomas in the Virgin Islands because it was one of the largest cruise ship ports in the world. Six months later I had my captain's license and my own charter sailboat. Then I became a licensed Coast Guard captain and earned my Divemaster rating."

After four years in the Virgin Islands and after three thousand dives and several underwater scuba outings showing tourists the local clear-water reefs, it was again time for a change of scene.

"I was healthy, happy, had a deep tan, and was bored. At that point, my now-wife, who was a diving instructor in the area, and I took the boat and sailed up to New York, where her family had a house with a slip in it. We parked the boat and pondered our next move. That's when I ended up in New York City working on animatronics, doing what I do now."

Today he divides his time between running his special effects shop and serving as the more recognizable and erudite half of *MythBusters*. It's the perfect partnership, where cohost Adam Savage provides the ebullient yin to Hyneman's analytical yang.

"Adam and I are two distinctly dissimilar people," says Jamie. "As anybody who watches the show can see, I'm the guy who is much more buttoned down and more methodical. I'm not very excitable; I'm relatively analytical in the way that I build. In contrast, Adam is all over the place. He's very animated. He's very impetuous. He's spontaneous. He's temperamental.

"The disparity of our characters turns out to be a real strength of the show, not just for entertainment value, but as a strong teaching method. Adam and I aren't afraid to express ourselves, even in our at times polar opposite fashions. What you get are two diametrically opposed outlooks, and when we focus on a single subject, that makes learning a lot easier and fun."

Although Jamie often feels off balance in his own shop around the chaotic antics of his partner, Adam, and executive producer, Rees, he's as driven and disciplined as ever. Hardware like linear servos and miniature rotary actuators are part of his routine, and if he can't find the proper machinery or technology to power a new animatronics project, he'll go ahead and invent something. As a result, Jamie holds two patents and has several patents pending.

"I'm just shy of fifty years old and I can still run circles around anybody here. I get up at four every morning, and after a couple hours of good solid workouts, I'm already through with the hardest part of my day. By the time I come to work on *MythBusters,* I'm coasting and floating on endorphins," he says.

Still, the strangest part of Jamie's life is his newfound recognition as a TV personality. Attesting to the power of television, Adam and Jamie are now regularly recognized and mobbed in public.

"As far as the fame, I've gone through stages with it. At first it was cool. 'I'm famous.' I get stopped when I walk on the sidewalk. Drivers honk their horns at me. People wanting autographs approach me in shopping malls. Recently I pulled into a restaurant parking lot and some kids spotted me and started running after me."

Still, being a famous MythBuster is all in a day's work.

"I've been on commercial shoots recently, unrelated to *MythBusters,* where it has been a problem. Passersby on the sidewalk would shout out 'MythBusters!' while we're in the middle of a sound shoot. I'm just a hired guy on the crew doing special effects, and the director asks, 'Who is this guy?' Then someone says, 'He's on Discovery Channel. He's one of the MythBusters.'"

Going down in the elevator of death, can a well-timed leap of faith save your skin?

The Elevator of Death

THE MYTH: What if the elevator you're riding suddenly plummets down the shaft? Can you save yourself at the very last second if you jump up as high as you can at the precise moment the elevator crashes to the ground?

THE PLAN: This experiment entailed two engineering challenges: First, figure out a way to raise and drop an elevator. Second, rig the victim—in this case, Buster, the crash test dummy—to jump up at just the right moment, and then measure his jump speed to see if he avoided what seemed like certain death.

To stage the experiment, the MythBusters located a derelict hotel in Oakland scheduled for demolition that had a nine-story elevator shaft. The elevator motor was nonfunctional, but the cabling (although a little rusty) was still intact after not having been operated in years. It was an ideal drop site—92 feet.

JAMIE: "This is another one of those circumstances where safety is incredibly important. We were right there. The falling elevator had a lot of torque in that place. It was dangerous. We have to constantly be alert that death is imminent in most every story that we do if we're not really paying full attention.

"But it's not about what you understand that can be dangerous in this kind of situation, it's about what you *don't* understand. But by the time we get to that final experiment, we've been thinking and working on it for about a month. We'll have extensive meetings and go through everything."

In addition to being cabled to a winch, all functioning elevator cars are normally linked to a counterweight, which weighs about the same as the car when half full. That keeps the system in balance so the car doesn't fall. But in order for the MythBusters to be able to drop the Elevator of Death, that counterweight system was gutted and eliminated.

PETER: "It wasn't just a thirty-five-hundred-pound elevator at play here. There was a thirty-five-hundred-pound counterweight, which was going in opposition. So if the elevator was at the bottom, then the counterweight was somewhere up near the top. Jamie and Adam had to eliminate the counterweight system. What really freaked me out was when Adam was standing in the elevator with a blowtorch cutting through the cables. We had to cut two of them to release the counterweight. What's going to happen? Will the elevator suddenly zoom to the top?"

Adam was in charge of rigging the well-worn elevator car so it could be raised to the top and dropped down. Jamie had the difficult job of figuring out how to get Buster to jump up at the last second inside the falling car. Instead of using gunpowder to spring Buster upward, he and his crew engineered a clever triple-spring pogo stick assembly on which Buster could sit on his way down the deadly shaft. The turbo-charged pogo launch would be triggered to jolt Buster upward during the final 6 feet of the elevator's plummet to earth.

Adam installed a 10,000-pound movie effects quick-release shackle between the cables at the top of the elevator car. As a result he could, on cue, yank the pin out from the shackle, causing the elevator to drop precipitously down the shaft. With the quick-release shackle installed and Buster seated inside on the turbo-charged pogo release unit, the MythBusters were ready to hoist the elevator to the top of the shaft. Bypassing the original motor, Jamie modified a robotic machine from his shop to hydraulically lift the 3,500-pound steel car to the very top floor.

ADAM: "The Elevator of Death was very intense from a safety perspective. When you think about how to drop an elevator, you have to rig it to a quick-release, which means there has to be a certain point in which you've brought the elevator to full height on a rope or a chain. Then you have to transfer it from that rope or chain to your quick-release. Now once you get it on the quick-release, nobody can go near that elevator shaft. Jamie and I thoroughly discussed the protocol as to who was allowed to be in the elevator shaft after we reached this code red."

The elevator, which hadn't moved in years, was dangling 90 feet in the air, ready for its final descent.

THE EXPERIMENT: With the quick-release mechanism attached and holding, and with Buster seated inside the elevator car, Adam waited at the top of the shaft for the

countdown. At the count of five, he would yank the linchpin free from the quick-release shackle, which in turn would separate the elevator from its cable and send the car crashing to its doom. In seconds, Buster would ride the car down nine floors, poised to jump off the pogo seat when the elevator was 6 feet from the bottom.

ADAM: "We were up at the top of that hotel, and the classic thing is when Peter and I have these moments, thinking, 'What the heck are we doing?' Either we're chasing otters away from grabbing Ping-Pong balls from a boat at the bottom of Monterey Bay or we're all standing there ready to escape from Alcatraz Island in a boat made out of raincoats, or with the Elevator of Death, I'm just about to pull on a cord that will drop this thirty-five-hundred-pound elevator down ten floors. I can't believe this is our job."

With Adam perched at the top of the shaft, Jamie and the rest of the crew stationed themselves in the basement. Ready to drop: 5-4-3-2-1.

Adam, both terrified and excited, pulled the cable that released the shackle pin. The elevator's rapid downward flight was brutally intense. It produced an enormous blast of air that shot through the old building, causing billowing clouds of dust in the basement. The entire shaft structure shook from the falling car's impact. The overhead cameras showed that Buster's pogo stick launch happened right on cue.

But did it save him?

THE RESULT: **PETER:** "Falling nine stories in that elevator probably had the same energy of a Mack truck doing fifty-five miles an hour on the road and running into a brick wall. There was no give in the floor. But the thing that really made Elevator of Death a great experiment was that it was a full-scale test. People will do small-scale testing with eggs and springs and little boxes. You can definitely prove the principle that way. And we could have dropped a heavy metal box from a high crane,

and it wouldn't have been any different. But we have to have the real thing! We don't really know what other forces are at work. There could have been a piston effect or air compressed under the elevator. All kinds of things could have gone on. We had to be authentic."

It was an unobstructed descent. By the bottom of the shaft, the elevator and Buster were freefalling at 53 mph. Buster jumped up at 3 feet per second—or 2 mph—with enough force to hit the roof. But he still hit the ground at a fatal speed of 51 mph.

An inspection of the downed elevator found poor Buster in several pieces. His head was severed from his body, and so were his arms. The results were not pretty for television's favorite crash test dummy.

ADAM: "This was more damage than we had ever done to Buster in one myth. Although Buster was well off the ground when the elevator smash-landed, a two-mile-an-hour jump was not enough to avoid the crash and keep him intact."

PETER: "The carnage was shocking; it was obvious from the first attempt that no one was going to walk away from a fall like that. We also included in the episode the story of the woman in the Empire State Building who was supposed to have fallen eighty-three floors in 1945 when a B17 plane went into the side of the building. It cut the ropes and the elevator just dropped. But from what we can understand, the elevator was slightly jammed in the shaft. Everyone said she fell eighty-three floors, but I don't think that's exactly true. We didn't get a chance to bust that myth on the show, but it's not true."

MYTH STATUS: BUSTED

JAMIE: "According to the laws of physics, a last-minute jump will not save you in a falling elevator. You might be weightless relative to the elevator, but you and the elevator are still going down at fifty-three miles an hour. Unless you can jump up at fifty-three miles an hour, you're in trouble."

ADAM: "I think this myth is definitely and finally busted."

SCIENTIFIC PRINCIPLE

PETER: "It's all about gravity. The misconception people have is when they jump up in the elevator, they think that they're getting zero g, and they're not. In relation to the car, you are getting a reduced g-force on your body, but in relation to planet Earth, you're falling at thirty-two feet per second per second. You'll hit the ground at fifty-five miles per hour, pull about three or four hundred g's of force, and you'll be dead."

The MythBusters are out to defy nature. Can a human survive 6 feet under— in the confines of a coffin?

Buried Alive!

THE MYTH: Can someone be mistakenly declared dead, put in a coffin, set into a grave, and be buried while still alive? Or is it merely gothic fiction?

ADAM: "Most of the macabre stories of being mistakenly buried alive belong to the dark days of medicine when pronouncing someone dead was a hit-or-miss kind of science."

MEDICAL NOTE

Today, to avoid such uncertainties, modern medicine follows five procedures before officially pronouncing someone dead.

1. Induce stimuli to see if there's any neurological response. (Many doctors take something like a car key and push very hard on the patient's thumbnail in order to induce pain.)

2. Using a penlight, check to see if the pupils react.

3. Listen for a heartbeat with a stethoscope.

4. Check for a pulse on the carotid artery.

5. Listen over both sides of the chest for any respirations. If a patient is not breathing and there's no pulse, that's considered evidence that the brain is not functioning.

THE PLAN: The plan was to bury Jamie alive. It would be a dangerous experiment, requiring an aboveground chamber and a casket strong enough to withstand tons of dirt. Several meters and instruments monitored Jamie's pulse and blood oxygen levels and the amount of potentially deadly CO_2 building up inside the casket. Asphyxiation was a real possibility, so two emergency medics were on hand at all times.

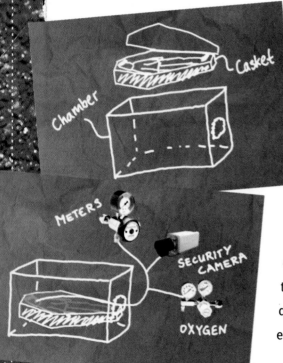

Chamber

Casket

METERS

SECURITY CAMERA

OXYGEN

JAMIE: "My coffin concerns were size, strength, and comfort. We decided on a coffin made of twenty-gauge steel over wood."

Buried inside the coffin along with Jamie were a carbon dioxide and oxygen meter, a pulse oxygen meter, a night vision camera, a microphone, a walkie-talkie, a thermometer, a humidity sensor, and an emergency supply of oxygen. The chamber was constructed to come apart easily if the team needed quick access to Jamie in the event of an emergency.

Since safety was the first priority, the casket was prepared for a trial run at the workshop. First, the casket was sealed with tape with Jamie inside. The monitoring systems were up and running, making sure he was okay. His blood level of carbon dioxide peaked at three percent. (Four percent is considered dangerous. Ten percent is lethal.)

ADAM: "More of us went inside the coffin to do the testing. We also tested it with me, Peter, and the researcher."

THE EXPERIMENT: The next step was to load Jamie inside the coffin and, using a forklift, lower him down into the aboveground grave, fill the chamber with earth, and carefully monitor Jamie's vital signs until he'd had enough. Jamie was apprehensive, hoping that the coffin wouldn't collapse under the extreme pressure of the dirt. In the workshop during the dry run, he lasted almost an hour inside the coffin. But outside there would be more "real" conditions to deal with.

JAMIE: "I felt increasingly more stressed, thereby producing more CO2, thus reducing my survival time inside the closed container."

Laid out in his casket, Jamie was about to undergo a rare ordeal. He would be buried alive!

JAMIE: "What set me off from the get-go was being up on the forklift with Adam and Peter at the controls. I'm twelve feet up in the air. I kept waiting for this big thud."

Adam gently lowered him into the burial chamber while the medics watched Jamie's vital signs closely.

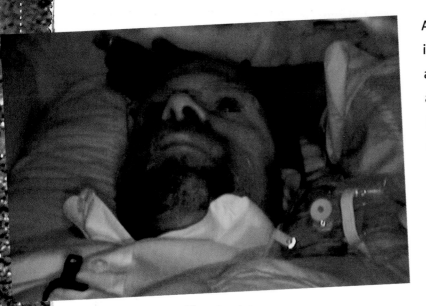

Any slight indication of acute stress, and he would be immediately exhumed. His heart rate, which started at a rate of 95 beats per minute, soon increased.

Then Jamie's temporary grave was covered with several tons of earth. The first Bobcat shovelful of dirt crushed the coffin a little bit, leaking dirt into the casket. Jamie's vital signs immediately showed his concern about the possibility of the coffin's lid slipping off the casket and crushing him.

JAMIE: "Once the casket was completely covered with dirt, it soon warped from the pressure. The corners popped up. I was thinking, 'Can the casket withstand the force pressing from above?'"

No more dirt was dumped. However, after the coffin began buckling more and changing shape, the experiment was halted.

JAMIE: "I was concerned. As the coffin was collapsing, I couldn't see what it was doing. I was visualizing things like the lid, as it starts to deform, moving off of its edge and punching in. Yet I speculated that eventually, when something crumples, it gets stronger, so it would get to the point where it wouldn't crush anymore."

Jamie lasted 30 humid minutes inside the casket, breathing only available air.

THE RESULT:

JAMIE: "I started panicking a little bit there at the end. While I don't have a fear of enclosed spaces at all, it was pretty scary. Feeling those walls starting to cave in, that really got me going, as I'm sure my pulse rate testified."

Jamie was right. At the point the experiment was halted and he was let out, his heart rate had jumped off the chart. Because of his accelerated pulse, Jamie used up a lot more oxygen.

PETER: "Unless you're claustrophobic, your heart rate gradually elevates. But we wanted to take it to the next step. Now that we have a baseline CO_2 increase, what happens if you woke up? It was fairly obvious from the results that we got with Jamie, as soon as the earth went over the coffin, Jamie's heart rate was going up. As soon as the coffin started to buckle, his heart rate was at one hundred twenty and the CO_2 increased and the respiration was going through the roof. That halved the amount of time he could stay in the coffin."

ADAM: "We got Jamie out of there in less than thirty seconds."

JAMIE: "It all turned out to be perfectly safe."

ADAM: "What are the chances of surviving six feet under? I don't think it's possible for *anyone* in a panicked state to survive a couple of hours being buried alive in a coffin that's crushing, let alone a couple of days later when they're exhumed and found to be alive. It's patently ridiculous."

Both Adam and Jamie agreed, the myth was extremely busted.

PETER: "Buried Alive myths are obviously very pervasive. We wanted to do the story, but we had to ask ourselves questions. How would we frame it? What experiment are we going to do? What was the point we were trying to make? Our point wasn't so much that you can't be buried alive in a coffin, it's that if you were, you'd probably not wake up, you'd die of CO_2 poisoning—even if you're in a comatose state—because you're still respirating. As soon as they seal the top of a coffin lid, whether it's a tight seal or not, and the CO_2 level starts going up, you would black out and die before you even left the mortuary."

SCIENTIFIC PRINCIPLE

PETER: "Simple scientific concept. Most people believe that you would run out of oxygen and that's why you'd die inside a coffin. In reality, you'd die much faster from CO_2 poisoning than you would from oxygen deprivation."

The MythBusters double as consumer safety sleuths to explore this dangerous candy-coated myth.

The Case of the Exploding Jawbreaker

THE MYTH: They're colorful, delicious, and fun, but can a simple candy like a large jawbreaker become a potential bomb?

JAMIE: "This is Peter's favorite story because he just loves jawbreakers."

THE PLAN: If somebody microwaves a large jawbreaker and nibbles on the outside, a crack can cause molten candy to burst out and cause painful burns. Exploding jawbreakers have been documented on television news and in police reports. The typical tale goes like this: A child microwaves a 3-inch jawbreaker, and then, when attempting to lick the hard candy, is injured by an explosion of hot liquid from within the jawbreaker. Children have suffered painful and severe burns—not dissimilar to chemical burns—on their faces and arms as a result of microwaved candies.

At the candy factory, mega-jawbreakers start out as one solid candy center and grow—much like snowballs—as different colors of sugar syrup are applied, layer by layer, in a process that takes five days.

PETER: "After we visited the jawbreaker factory and found out that a jawbreaker takes five days to make, we realized it takes as many days to make as it takes to suck."

When Jamie cut a jawbreaker in half and saw the multiple layers of hard candy, he realized that when the hardened sugar syrup was heated or microwaved, there was clear potential for a phenomenon called "temperature differential," which means that one of the interior layers of the jawbreaker could heat more rapidly than its hard outer shell. An inner layer could then expand to create internal pressure and instability.

To reenact the incident of the exploding jawbreaker, the MythBusters team first built a model of a mouth that was capable of chewing a heated jawbreaker. The artificial mouth was constructed from old dentures. Just as in a human mouth, the bottom jaw was hinged so it could move up and down, while the upper jaw remained stationary. Actual-sized steel teeth were cast and welded into the upper and lower jaws. Then, with a tool called a digital force gauge, a steel rod was attached to the jaw assembly and adjusted to give the jaws a maximum bite force of 170 pounds, replicating the actual bite pressure of a real mouth.

ADAM: "Next, after trying out various microwave settings from defrost to reheat, the MythBusters came up with the ideal heating and cooling regimen to create a potential exploding jawbreaker. Using an infrared thermometer, its molten sugar inner core retained heat up to a dangerous two hundred twenty-five degrees!"

Adam and Jamie quickly loaded the highly unstable jawbreaker onto their steel jaw contraption and got ready for the big crunch. The heated jawbreaker actually did blast open. In seconds Adam caught fragments of hot jawbreaker, causing a minor burn on his arm.

The MythBusters proved conclusively that one large jawbreaker plus microwave plus steel chomping teeth equals scalded MythBusters.

THE RESULT:

ADAM: "If you're a five-year-old kid and this went off in your face, there's no doubt it would leave serious burns on you. I could still feel it ten to fifteen seconds later. It wasn't cooling down."

Adam and Jamie explored two additional options in recreating high-heat-retention exploding jawbreakers.

For one experiment, they ground the jawbreaker into a powderlike substance and combined it with caustic soda, which is often used in the cleaning of food processing equipment. The concoction was put inside a microwave on high for five minutes. The result was a highly combustible molten hot ash material.

And for one more try, Adam and Jamie kept the mega-jawbreaker inside its clear plastic packaging and stuck it inside a toaster oven to simulate the effect of being left in the sun for a few hours. Although they could not reproduce a biting explosion, under radiant heat the jawbreaker was still molten in the middle and crispy on the outside.

MYTH STATUS: CONFIRMED

ADAM: "This myth is confirmed, confirmed, confirmed. And dangerous. Don't try any of these experiments at home. You could end up burned!

"This was one myth where we came up with three likely scenarios, and all three turned out to be equally plausible."

SCIENTIFIC PRINCIPLE

⚛ **PETER:** "This experiment had excellent pieces of science having to do with differential heating and thermodynamics in relation to the ability of an object to retain heat."

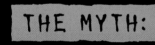

Running through raindrops: Are the MythBusters on the level or are they all wet?

Is It Worth Running in the Rain?

51

THE PLAN: In order to answer this mythical query, the MythBusters recreated controlled conditions involving the velocity of rain.

ADAM: "The setup included a one-hundred-foot-long indoor course, which Jamie and I walked through—and then ran through—during a simulated downpour of homemade rain. In order to accurately perform the experiment, we manufactured some precise precipitation. Then, while both walking *and* running, we wore identical cotton coveralls, which were then weighed after each test to see how much water they had soaked up."

In order to gain consistent and reliable results, the trickiest part of the process, according to Jamie, was getting a reliable and consistent rain—something realistic, with the proper velocity, the right raindrop size, and an even spread of rainfall over the entire hundred-foot distance. When taking their test jaunts, Adam and Jamie also had to make sure their perspiration wouldn't mix with the rain and taint the data. So both elected to wear something snug and form-fitting underneath their coveralls—skintight latex outfits.

Terminal Velocity
22 fps 60

MAXIMUM SPEED! 147

PETER: "How big is a raindrop? Rain has to fall from a certain height before it actually becomes a raindrop. It breaks up once it gets to a certain speed. It has a certain velocity. It hits the ground at a certain rate. Then there's the question of, How hard is the rain falling? What's average rainfall (which we concluded might be one and a half to two inches per hour)? It's an incredibly detailed experiment, which is often the case. Things you think will be very simple turn out to be extremely difficult and have a huge number of variables."

Using a hose and squirting water downward wasn't going to simulate real rainfall, so the next step was to buy the necessary piping in order to build a man-made downpour system. Adam's rain system needed to generate actual raindrops that could achieve terminal velocity. (Note: After falling 60 feet, a drop of water travels at a maximum speed of nearly 22 feet per second, after which a drop cannot go any faster, no matter how far it plummets toward the Earth.)

Adam's rain delivery system was located inside an abandoned military hangar. It was comprised of 150 feet of pipe with sprinkler heads installed every 6 feet. Jamie supplied the water by legally tying into a nearby fire hydrant. The MythBusters then learned that accessing water is one thing, but getting it to travel 60 feet straight up into the air is quite another.

JAMIE: "According to my calculations, the water needed to be pumped at fifteen pounds per square inch in order to simulate a real rainstorm. Fortunately, we were able to secure a pump capable of pumping up to fifty-five pounds per square inch."

With Adam's pipes and sprinkler heads in place, and Jamie's water pumping, the MythBusters gave their rainy course its first dry run. After a few short test rains, they achieved precisely the amount of rainfall they were looking for—between 2 and 3 inches an hour. Digital gauges were then set out along the 100-foot walking/running course to verify the rainfall. On some of the tests, the MythBusters added wind, using fans, as a variable.

Finally, it was time to begin the tests.

THE EXPERIMENT:

ADAM: "Step one was to make the rain more visible by using red dye. Step two was to put on the coveralls. [Each pair weighed approximately 757 grams.] Step three was to find an answer to this age-old mystery: Is it better to walk or run in the rain? A high-speed camera running at a thousand frames per second captured every single step and raindrop."

JAMIE: "We each walked the eighteen-second course twice, once with wind, once without. Each take was timed, and then the coveralls were immediately removed and set onto the scales. After both his walks, Adam's coveralls weighed in at seven hundred eighty-five grams. After my walks, the coveralls soaked in almost the same amount of water."

What happened when Adam and Jamie picked up the pace and ran? Adam's coveralls weighed in at around 798 grams. On Jamie's run, the difference wasn't as great: The coveralls weighed 793 grams. But surprisingly, the MythBusters' raw data pointed to an answer that flew in the face of common sense. It makes a difference whether you walk or run.

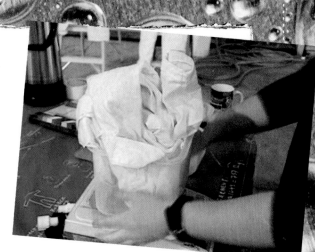

THE RESULT:

PETER: "This was another story where we went and interviewed experts from National Oceanographic Atmospheric Administration. They had done a test wherein they went out into the rain and ran a course that was roughly one hundred feet. They came up with the conclusion that it's better to run because you spend less time in the rain. But our results were totally counterintuitive. It was better to walk. We were the first to actually try to build controlled rain with a hundred-foot sprinkler system in this

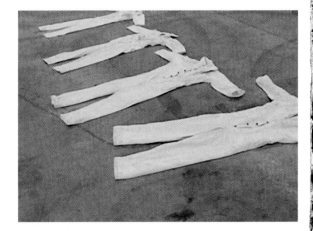

forty-eight-foot-tall building that was used for painting airplanes out at Alameda. You could see their minds turning at the NOAA: 'Yes, that's right. The arms become horizontal surfaces and so do the legs when you're running. And horizontal surfaces, obviously, catch more rain.'"

MYTH STATUS: BUSTED

ADAM: "The results weren't what I'd expected at all. Over that distance, our data showed that it was actually better to walk because you were presenting less of a surface for the rain. It was mostly falling on your shoulders and your head, whereas if you are running, you're also taking drops on the front. Our suits showed a huge amount of moisture on our legs—when you run you make your legs go vertically higher."

JAMIE: "It's better to walk than run. It was very clear. On a hundred-foot course with two to three inches of rain delivery per hour, we got more rain per foot running than we did while walking. This myth is busted. It's better to walk than to run in the rain."

SCIENTIFIC PRINCIPLE

ADAM: "To me, running in the rain is the single best example of how difficult it is to scientifically frame a simple question. Over a certain period of time, everybody experiences the same amount of wetness. How do you even determine how long to run? Because arbitrarily it's entirely possible that at a hundred fifty feet, it's better to run. If you had a grant to test it, you would have to test it over fifty, a hundred, a hundred fifty, two hundred, three hundred feet, walking, running at different average paces with both men and women. Different storm cycles and wind conditions. It's never as simple as it seems. We'd love to have the time to go out there and do that test for three or four more days and try to do all those and show the graphs."

PETER: "Everything that we do—and I can't emphasize this enough—is based on exactly what you would do in a scientific study, which is to look at the previous research and look at the things they took into consideration. The more you can reproduce what someone else has done and go from there, the better your results will be."

The MythBusters delve into one of the most thrilling historical escape reenactments ever attempted on television.

Escape from Alcatraz

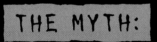

THE MYTH: Did three inmates from the infamous Alcatraz Federal Prison successfully escape off the island on a handmade raft and vanish without a trace?

HISTORICAL NOTE

It's the greatest mystery in the twenty-nine-year history of Alcatraz Federal Prison, located in San Francisco Bay. On June 11, 1962, Frank Morris and two brothers, Clarence and John Anglin, successfully escaped from the prison and the island of Alcatraz. The National Park Service web site, www.nps.gov/alcatraz, has assessed the chance that the three survived as "very questionable." Convicted bank robbers, Morris and the Anglin brothers had busted out of "the Rock," but they disappeared off the face of the earth. What are the chances they made it out alive?

Officially, no one ever escaped Alcatraz and lived to tell the tale. Prior to the trio's attempt, thirty-six prisoners were involved in escapes. Seven were shot and killed, two drowned, five were unaccounted for, and the rest were captured. Two convicts made it off the island and were returned. Morris and the Anglin brothers are not officially credited as having successfully escaped.

Caged in five-by-nine-foot cells, Morris and the Anglins chipped through their ventilation grills using spoons. When the escapees burrowed out of their cells, they found themselves in an empty service shaft. Leaving dummies behind in their beds (with plaster heads and hair made of paintbrush bristles) to ward off evening prisoner counts, night after night the plotters scrambled out into the unmonitored walkway. From there they climbed up pipes three floors to the cellblock roof. For months, in the pitch-black of night—and remarkably, without making the slightest noise that might alert guards (who were within easy visual range from the gun galleries)—they constructed an inflatable raft from fifty stolen rubber raincoats. Using rubber cement adhesive from the prison hobby shop, they glued together several rubber squares to form their getaway craft. Oar paddles were made from stray pieces of wood.

During the day, Morris and his accomplices studied the ebb and flow of the bay tides. On the night of their escape, the three grabbed the raft and oars from the rooftop, then climbed back down 50 feet to the ground. They scurried to the shore, a remarkable distance to carry all that gear right under the nose of the law.

The swirling tidal currents were more feared than any wall. At the cold water's edge, Morris and the Anglin brothers pumped up their raft using a converted accordion and off they

MYTHBUSTERS

went. Ten hours passed before they were discovered missing, after which a major manhunt comprised of FBI agents, coast guard, highway patrol, sheriff's deputies, and local police scoured the Bay Area. An inmate named Alan West told the FBI that the escapees' plan had been to paddle the raft north to Angel Island, then hit the mainland from there.

But neither the men nor the raft were ever found. Two paddles later washed up on the bay shore.

The modern legend remains: Did Morris—an accomplished escape artist with an IQ of 133—and the Anglin brothers pull off one of the greatest prison breaks in history? Or did the escapees drown in the shark-infested San Francisco Bay, as Alcatraz law enforcement experts postulate? Using ingenuity and common sense, Adam and Jamie pursued their greatest challenge as MythBusters.

ADAM: "When we first began researching, we found out that the San Francisco Maritime Museum had obtained some of the pieces of evidence of the original escape from the FBI. The museum allowed us to come down, and they put the samples out for us. We had already read all eighteen hundred pages of the FBI report on the escape, which included detailed drawings of all the pieces they had found—one life jacket, two paddles, and a small pouch of photographs of one of the guys' families."

PETER: "Watching all the films on the escape, including Clint Eastwood's *Escape from Alcatraz,* it surprised me that up until now, no one attempted to reconstruct the raft. One professional swimmer tried to swim to Angel Island, but he didn't make it. Clint Eastwood's character was floating on an air-filled pontoon with their bodies mostly in the water. I'd never seen an accurate reproduction, not even on *America's Most Wanted.* To me, building the raft seemed the most obvious thing to do, to see if it could be done. We're told the FBI performs these reconstructions all the time."

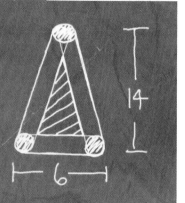

During their visit to Alcatraz Island and the prison cellblock, Adam and Jamie witnessed firsthand how crumbled and eaten away the cell walls were, due to the dampness of the cold and moist island atmosphere. The MythBusters were easily able to squirm through open holes in individual cells that landed them in adjoining unmonitored corridors.

Once they were confident that Morris and the Anglins could venture in and out of their jail cells in the dark of night, it was time to reconstruct the escape raft. According to FBI intelligence, the rubber rainwear raft was 14 feet long and 6 feet wide. It was a triangular pontoon model with only a single-layer rubber rainwear floor to separate the escapees from the sharks below.

Adam and Jamie cut the rubber raincoat material into evenly measured squares. To make sure the raft would be airtight, each seam was glued, dried, and compressed. Making the three pontoons meant rolling each piece of rubber up like a rug and sealing the ends. The last step was to build the floor of the raft and glue it around the triangular pontoon frame. An old accordion squeezebox was converted into an air pump. Using a Ping-Pong ball, Jamie engineered an ingenious one-way valve so the squeezebox could blow air in without it being sucked back out again.

It took thirty raincoats for Adam and Jamie to reproduce the escape raft. The easiest part, they found, was to assemble the three wooden paddles, and the MythBusters crew was ready to set sail across the choppy tides of San Francisco Bay.

In planning their own escape from the Rock, Adam and Jamie questioned the original assumption that the three escapees paddled north to Angel Island, as convict Alan West had declared. To sail the raft to Angel Island would have meant traveling against strong windy tides. The normal currents would have routed the handmade raft westerly toward the Golden Gate Bridge and out to sea. Adam and Jamie suspected that the convicts knew this beforehand.

ADAM: "Peter had been sailing San Francisco Bay a lot. He understood that the currents from Alcatraz to Angel Island were super fast. So he came up with the possibility that if they went from the north shore of the Golden Gate Bridge *with* the current, all they had to do was paddle about a quarter mile north and the currents would carry them all the way to the Marin Headlands. I think they were smart enough to have counted on the tides, using them to their advantage."

PETER: "Anyone serving time on Alcatraz could see the currents from every angle of the island. But the best view could be seen walking from the exercise yard to the Hall of Industry. Plus, you could walk right onto the edge of the island. There were no fences or anything. Not only that, but the inmates used to man the boats that went to and from the island. Having kayaked out into the bay, it was obvious to me that if we went into the bay, we could use the currents to our advantage, not to our disadvantage, by working against them. Clearly, if those guys had put as much thought as they had into

their escape—and it *was* incredibly well thought out—we assumed that they would have applied the same level of scrutiny to the actual voyage across the bay as they did to the escape from the island."

JAMIE: "They were clever about this whole thing from the get-go, including how they got the materials in the first place and where they assembled it, right under the nose of the guards. It was all very well planned out, so it's only logical to assume that they gave a fair amount of thought to the tide patterns as well."

To further study the best escape route from Alcatraz, Adam and Jamie visited an engineering facility called the Bay Models, a research center that houses a remarkable scale model of the entire San Francisco Bay. The Bay Models itself covers nearly two acres and can duplicate a full day's tidal movement in less than fifteen minutes. According to scientists there, the model site very accurately replicates the tides, currents, and motions of the bay.

PETER: "I live near the Bay Models, so I went down one weekend by

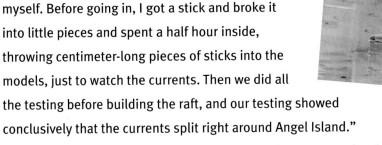

myself. Before going in, I got a stick and broke it into little pieces and spent a half hour inside, throwing centimeter-long pieces of sticks into the models, just to watch the currents. Then we did all the testing before building the raft, and our testing showed conclusively that the currents split right around Angel Island."

After launching a miniature craft numerous times across the simulated high-tide course, the MythBusters found that the model raft repeatedly drifted from Alcatraz west toward a shoreline called the Marin Headlands at the northern end of the Golden Gate Bridge. Judging from the Bay Models, Adam and Jamie surmised that paddling north against the tides to Angel Island was an impossible task.

ADAM: "Despite what they told other prisoners, maybe Angel Island was never in the plan at all. There's no way that they could make it to Angel Island."

JAMIE: "I think they actually took advantage of the currents and got on them like a river, headed toward the Golden Gate Bridge, and specifically the north side of the Golden Gate Bridge at the Marin Headlands, where they could easily make it to shore."

PETER: "What didn't get into the show was if you leave from the southern side of Alcatraz, where a lot of the escapees apparently left from, the current takes you directly to the southern part of the bridge. However, if you leave from the northern side, which is where these guys left from, it takes you mid-span, or closer to the Marin Headlands. So I thought, just do what you do in a kayak when you paddle across a river flow. As long as you keep paddling north, which is easy because you can see the Golden Gate Bridge right there as a landmark, the current will do all the work for you."

The decision was made. The MythBusters would follow the natural tides and float their escape raft in a westerly direction from Alcatraz Island to the Marin Headlands, a route of a little over 3 miles.

THE EXPERIMENT:

Roughly forty years after the original escape, the MythBusters aimed to prove that a successful escape from Alcatraz could very well have happened. But forget Angel Island. In the dead of night at high tide, the MythBusters were going to paddle across the San Francisco Bay and reach land around the Marin Headlands.

Since three men engineered the original escape, Adam and Jamie enlisted a MythBusters workshop assistant to be their companion for the voyage. While Adam and Jamie wore actual prison coveralls (and no life jackets) to make the journey, the assistant was dressed in a buoyant wet suit so that he could immediately help the guys if anything went wrong. All three wore strobe locator lights, and a camera crew, paramedics, and a trained lifeguard would follow the little raft to freedom.

On the northwest edge of Alcatraz, the high tide was rushing out at more than 3 knots, while the wind blew at 5 knots. The water was just over 60 degrees. The conditions were identical to those Morris and the Anglin brothers faced on that fateful night in June 1962. Adam was only a little optimistic about their chances of success.

ADAM: "I gave us a sixty percent chance of making it, a twenty percent chance of immediate catastrophic failure, and a twenty percent slow descent into the depths."

As Jamie climbed in, nobody really knew how the raft would react under such extreme seafaring conditions. Soon Adam and Will climbed aboard and the journey was under way. The raft had passed its first test by sustaining the weight of all three men.

If the MythBusters miscalculated their operation as they paddled furiously west, they faced the danger of the currents sweeping them under the bridge and out into the Pacific Ocean. They risked hypothermia, drowning, or worse, shark attacks.

At first they lost sight of Alcatraz Island when a large tanker blocked their view. Then the raft began to get weaker. Every ten minutes they had to add more air, and as the waves got rougher, they continually bailed water out of the tiny raft. Were they still on course?

After forty minutes cramped inside the raft, there were still no major leaks. The pontoons were undamaged. The journey began shaping up well. Alcatraz was back in sight, and the Marin Headlands lay just ahead. After 3 miles of maneuvering rushing tides and choppy waves, the raincoat raft landed safely on the beach of the headlands, making landfall just east of the northern structure of the Golden Gate Bridge. The MythBusters' running days were over.

PETER: "Because the boat following with the lighting couldn't get close enough to the shore, we had to light the final sequence with a flashlight, just the second cameraman and me with a penlight. It was completely pitch black. None of the boats could get anywhere near the shoreline. That's why there's only one shot of Adam yelling, 'We made it.'"

ADAM: "Here's the classic Adam and Jamie dichotomy. After we made it all the way across the bay and we're just about there, we're met by one of the motorboats from the mother ship that was following us. Jamie decides to get into that boat and go back to the mother ship. I thought, *Are you kidding? I want to make it from Alcatraz to land.* Close wasn't good enough. Stepping onto land . . . *that* was thrilling."

THE RESULT: At first it seemed improbable, but the MythBusters truly engineered their own successful prison escape. If Morris and the Anglins had followed the same course, they too would have made it to dry land. Because of Adam and Jamie's alternate crossing, the Escape from Alcatraz myth had added credibility.

PETER: "Everything we did was authentic. We had authentic uniforms made of the same materials. We escaped at exactly the same time of year, at the same time of day, with the same water temperature, the same air temperature, and the same wind speed. We lucked out in that every single parameter was exactly the same. We not only filled the raft with Jamie and Adam, but also with a third person who was specifically selected so that their total weight matched that of the three escaping prisoners. Whenever we can replicate an experiment to that extreme level, where we feel we've nailed every aspect, it's incredibly satisfying. We proved you could make the trip in fifty minutes and that those guys could have been halfway up Highway 101 by dawn. Whether or not they made it was not the point, as far as we were concerned."

If the escapees did make it ashore, they immediately blended into humanity without leaving a trace. According to FBI files, no cars were reported stolen and no phone calls to potential contacts were made. Rumor has it that there were later sightings of the escapees in New Orleans, Washington, DC, and even in Florida playing golf. But if Morris and the Anglins became fugitives instead of shark bait, none of them ever came forward to brag about it.

PETER: "Another thing that didn't get into the show, which we thought was critical, was that the pieces of debris that were found were found on the west side of Angel Island. The only way the debris would have gotten there was if it were released from Horseshoe Bay on the north shore, the Marin Headlands, where we landed."

MYTH STATUS: CONFIRMED

ADAM: "The myth is confirmed. Given a reasonable amount of intelligence, I think it's entirely possible that they made it. Again, the most critical evidence that they didn't is the fact that no one's heard from them since."

JAMIE: "Unless they find any specific evidence that these guys lived happily ever after once they got ashore, we won't know whether it was true or not. But we now know it could be done."

ADAM: "While these guys were supposed to be bright, and while the amount of work they did was amazing, the Anglin brothers were in jail for

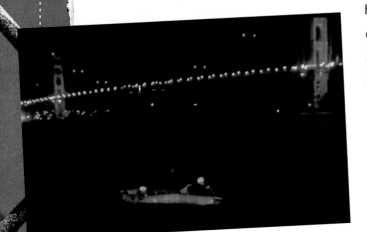

having cased a bank in a town of about four hundred people driving in a brand-new convertible Cadillac. The next day they robbed the bank in the same Caddy. It apparently took all of about forty-five minutes to catch them. So while Frank Morris might have had a high IQ, the others definitely weren't the sharpest tools in the shed. All three guys, Morris and the Anglin brothers, spent most of their lives behind bars, so they knew jail well, and the idea that these three could have made it is definitely plausible. The idea that all three evaded the law for the next fifty years . . . I don't think so."

PETER: "Personally, I think they escaped and got away with it."

Are Adam and Jamie junkies, or just junk food junkies? Can eating poppy seed bagels and cakes the morning before a job interview drug test cause you to test positive?

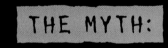

Poppy Seed Drug Test

THE MYTH: Eating poppy seed bagels or poppy seed cake in the morning will cause you to test positive on a drug screen.

The MythBusters obtained some poppy seed bagels and poppy seed cake, and a bunch of urine test containers and drug-testing kits. Adam gorged himself on poppy seed cake; Jamie consumed a few poppy seed bagels. No other food was eaten. Both drank lots of water in order to serve up a half-dozen urine samples. Jamie and Adam were then screened for heroin use with the drug-testing kits (obtained over the Internet). The tests were conducted after one hour, two hours, four hours, eight hours, and the following morning.

THE EXPERIMENT: **ADAM:** "The urine tests used were amino acid tests, which meant that the tests contained antibodies directed toward a specific compound, in this case codeine and the morphine in the urine. Heroin is broken down to those two substances. While poppy seeds have codeine and morphine in them, they are in very low concentrations, which explains why people don't get any physical or mental effects from opiates eating poppy seeds."

Initial tests before any eating or drinking showed the MythBusters clear of opiates. Then, half an hour after eating the poppy seed products, Jamie and Adam conducted their second drug test. Adam tested positive for opiates. Jamie, who ate much less—only three poppy seed bagels—tested positive as well.

ADAM: "I'm impressed that it metabolized that fast. Each test was supposed to be able to detect between three hundred and twelve hundred nanograms (or billionths) of a gram of codeine. At those levels, however, there was no way to distinguish between poppy seeds and heroin use."

JAMIE: "Unfortunately, none of the drug testing manufacturers offered a service that double-checked false-positive tests. Since many have lost their jobs through false-positive tests— some without knowing, due to a pre-employment test—in the future perhaps pre-employment testers should consider including a screening test first. Then if a test is positive, they could move on to a more accurate form of testing, like a gastro mass spectrometer, which unfortunately also has its limitations."

THE RESULT:

Four hours after consumption, the MythBusters still tested positive for opiates. Eight hours later they were still positive. So how long did the MythBusters come up with false-positive tests? Eighteen hours later, the effects of the poppy seeds seemed to wear down, and Jamie and Adam finally tested negative again.

MYTH STATUS: CONFIRMED

JAMIE: "This myth is clearly true. We ate a normal amount of poppy seed products and they showed positive on the test for a fairly long period of time. Past studies have shown that false-positive tests are capable of showing up for seventy-two hours."

PETER: "It's not about busting the drug-testing companies here. They put a warning on their products [regarding accuracy]. It's more about busting the  people who apply these kinds of tests in pre-employment screening. Poppy seeds are not the only things that can mess up a test. There are normal medications that will give false readings, and the employer does not have to disclose the results. It had quite a political slant. Our demographic wants to know about this stuff, and when we put those stories to air, they really like it. We want to do a whole round of product testing, because there are lots out there that are dangerous and misleading."

ADAM: "In the whole history of *MythBusters*, this is the only myth that we ever completed in a single day."

The MythBusters get medieval. Can they turn a log into a lethal weapon?

Medieval Tree Cannon

The MythBusters get medieval. Can they turn a log into a lethal weapon?

THE MYTH: This one comes from medieval times. It involves a Hungarian tribe called Pachish, which was threatened by its neighbors. The entire tribe got together, and in one night, they made a cannon out of a tree. They shot off the cannon using gunpowder, but the cannon exploded, killing half the townspeople.

THE PLAN: To test this myth, Jamie and Adam set out to build a tree cannon to see if it would explode when fired. Tree cannons were used in fourteenth-century England and as recently as a hundred years ago in eastern Europe. In order to make theirs, Adam and Jamie needed a large European hardwood log. They picked out a piece of English elm that weighed several hundred pounds.

Since people living in medieval Hungary didn't have power tools, the MythBusters fashioned their tools after examining a thousand-year-old toolbox found in Sweden. Jamie stripped the log's bark with an axe. Adam fashioned a medieval saw out of a forklift pallet. Jamie also forged an authentic spoon drill, just like one of the first drills ever used, in order to drill a barrel through the center of the log.

Next, the MythBusters put five solid iron bands around the log body to help the tree cannon absorb each blast. The rings were forged and heated in a furnace, hammered out, pulled tight while still red-hot, and riveted into place. After being riveted in and cooled with water, the bands shrunk tightly around the log. A barrel was drilled through the body of the cannon using Jamie's spoon drill. By Jamie's estimation, it would have taken two days to manually drill the 5-foot barrel.

ADAM: "Since the myth states that the cannon was drilled overnight, technically, the myth was busted. Yet after Jamie hand-chiseled a round cannonball from a block of granite, we tested the rest of this explosive myth by

finishing the cannon our way, using modern drilling equipment.
After completing the tree cannon, a crude batch of medieval gunpowder was mixed and formulated, but for safety reasons, the fuse was lit electronically from a distance."

THE EXPERIMENT:

While the replica cannon fired beautifully, the myth still stated that the tree cannon blew up when fired. Starting with 3-ounce cartridges of gunpowder, a tennis ball was squeezed down the cannon's barrel. Soon after an electric igniter was taped into place and ignited, the tennis ball was long gone. So was Jamie's hand-carved cannon ball, which was fired next. The medieval tree cannon remained intact.

PETER: "When we blew up the cannon at the end, we put five pounds of powder into that thing. We were told to stand away, and we asked the pyrotechnician where he

would be. He was a hundred and fifty feet away. I was standing next to him when that thing went off. It exploded into pieces. The metal bands around the cannon were never seen again. They must have flown at least three hundred feet into the bay."

MYTH STATUS: PLAUSIBLE

The MythBusters proved that a working cannon can be made out of a tree, and they also showed that the Hungarian townsfolk could have been wiped out when the tree cannon exploded.

SCIENTIFIC PRINCIPLE

PETER: "The principle is whether you can contain an explosion inside a wooden object. There's also a historical dimension in that it turns out that tree cannons have been made, and quite successfully so. There are specific aspects to do with ballistics, like what angle you're laying the cannon for maximum distance. What is the relative bore of it? Ultimately we could have probably made the walls a lot thinner. We were probably overly cautious."

SAFETY NOTE

☠ Using a premeasured charge of gunpowder packed in aluminum foil to fashion a small cartridge, even though this qualifies as a blank, is still a dangerous business when shooting a cannon. Once a cannon is loaded, nobody should get in front of the muzzle. Inserting a fuse that touches the powder inside fires the cannon. Is it possible to put too much powder in a cannon? Certainly. The cannon could get overstressed and blow up. Don't try this at home!

ADAM: "We're often dealing with a set of parameters that people have never dealt with before. We're often outside of the experiential range of the experts that we deal with, particularly the Hollywood pyrotechnicians. They're used to Hollywood explosions that look spectacular, but are only minimally dangerous to stage."

PETER: "Most really dangerous explosions don't look like much at all. They may be a puff of smoke, but what you hear is the sound of bits of metal flying through the air. It's not the actual explosion. The typical pyrotechnician is used to throwing up a big bag of gasoline that ignites and looks great on the set. He doesn't often get to put five pounds of gunpowder into a tree cannon and blow it up. He might have no idea what's going to happen, whereas I would rather trust Jamie specifically. There are checks and balances between the three of us. There are a lot of dissenting opinions, and we'll discuss things until we're all happy."

ADAM: "Actually, we found the FBI bomb squad to be the safest pyros we've ever worked with."

JAMIE: "The pyros come in as experts. 'You can't do this, you can do that. This is safe, and this isn't.' But they don't always know. We figure if they say it's okay to put more explosives in, then it's okay. But they're human, and we all make misjudgments. We've learned to be more cautious. It's up to us to acquire the knowledge we need outside our realm."

Does a sinking ship create a powerful drag on those close by in the water? A *Titanic*-sized legend asks the question, will a sinking ship suck you down as it goes under?

Down with the Mythtanic!

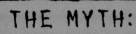

THE MYTH: **ADAM:** "There's a myth that says that if you're on a ship when it's sinking, it will suck you down with it. The myth further states that if a large ship sinks, passengers need to swim or row as far away as they possibly can, because as the ship goes down, a tremendous suction will draw everyone and everything down with it."

JAMIE: "Three different mythical *Titanic* theories prevailed that would explain such a phenomenon. One, that air mixes in with the water as it rushes up from the boat, making the water less dense, making you fall through the water quicker. Two, that the cavities in the ship will create an area for the water to rush in, which will pull you into the ship. Three, a ship moving rapidly down through the water toward the bottom of the sea will create a vortex above it, sucking you in."

Before trying this experiment out on a real boat, the MythBusters applied all three theories in a midsize experiment using a local 12-foot diving pool. They wanted to isolate which of the three forces would be in play when a shiplike object sank. Using a homemade hydrometer, a simple flotation device designed to measure the specific gravity or density of a liquid, and a weighted wooden box meant to simulate a sinking ship, the MythBusters measured the water's density by noting how far the hydrometer bobbed up and down when a bubble machine and the sinking object aerated the water. In a smaller experiment, suction was dramatically created as Adam rode a vortex to the bottom of the pool. Would the real thing—a full-sized boat—create the same suction effect on a full-sized scale?

ADAM: "A rugged nine-ton steel boat was drafted for the full-sized experiment, and we learned that sinking a boat wasn't easy. So we drilled holes in the boat below the waterline, holes that could be replaced with threaded fittings, enabling it to be resealed. Then the boat was towed to a dry dock site. A cabled harness attached to a crane was then rigged to the boat,

making it easier to bring the boat back up for further 'sinkings.'"

Dubbed *Mythtanic,* the MythBusters' sunken vessel was now ready for its launching (or should we say, its sinking). Jamie's checkered past working in the Caribbean as a diver, salvager, and an underwater guide was about to come in handy. After some scuba breathing lessons, Adam was also ready for the experiment.

THE EXPERIMENT:

The *Mythtanic* proved to be one of the MythBusters' most dangerous stunts. A crew of dry dock workers helped to sink the boat and then recover it. Most had heard of the myth but agreed that there were other dangers to consider besides being sucked down. The weather was cold. Visibility was uncertain, as currents stirred the cold water into a murky blur. The *Mythtanic* would sink right under a huge crane so that the boat could be rescued back from the deep again and again if necessary.

After opening just one hole below, the water rushed in quickly. As the *Mythtanic* sank for the first time, Adam panicked and bailed from the deck early, jumping off the boat before it sank 40 feet below into the murk—though Jamie held his ground.

ADAM: "Not knowing whether it could suck me down was absolutely one of the most frightening things ever. I had no idea whether or not I would be sucked in. That's why it took two tries. You're standing on a vessel that weighs about twenty-eight thousand pounds, as much as a loaded Mack truck. Your body experiences the mass, momentum, and the movement. When it starts to move in ways that it shouldn't, like the very first time it started to roll, I freaked out."

PETER: "I was on board as well, filming from the front, when I suddenly saw Jamie's hand reaching out to try to grab Adam to pull him back into the zone. But he was gone."

JAMIE: "Actually, my hand was out there because I didn't want to get too far away from Adam in case he got pulled down."

ADAM: "The speed of descent was fast, and while I knew my job was to stay with the boat and feel the suction, my sense of survival kicked in at a critical moment."

PETER: "To me, *Mythtanic* was potentially our most dangerous story. You're standing on this boat, you're in the bay, and it's pitch-black. Jamie is coming back up from the bottom saying he's getting ice headaches because of the temperature of the water. While the boat took ages to fill, once it went, it sank immediately. The thought of being caught on a boat in the middle of the ocean, going down when you can't see a thing, was frightening."

JAMIE: "I was down there and it took every ounce of my strength to pull these cables together underwater. I had no visibility while I was lugging this huge cable. I was cold and totally disoriented. I held on to a rail for support."

ADAM: "Everybody made fun of me, all of the longshoremen at the San Francisco dry dock. But even though there was a lot of ribbing because I jumped off the first time, they all agreed that none of them would have been foolish enough [to stay on board]."

THE RESULT: In a second take, Adam and Jamie stood on board as the boat sank. Was anyone pulled down with the ship in a vortex? While bravely staying on board and going down with his ship, Adam felt no suction whatsoever.

ADAM: "The second time the boat went down, I was a little more confident that it wouldn't suck me down. Plus, I couldn't have been more central to the boat where it went down. The entire boat just dropped underneath me. As I hit the water up to my neck, I never went any lower."

MYTH STATUS: BUSTED

Unlike the midsize test in the swimming pool where a vortex *was* created, a real boat has a much larger surface area and is unable to go down fast enough to create such a vortex. And while there are many reasons to swim away from a sinking boat, none of them involve suction.

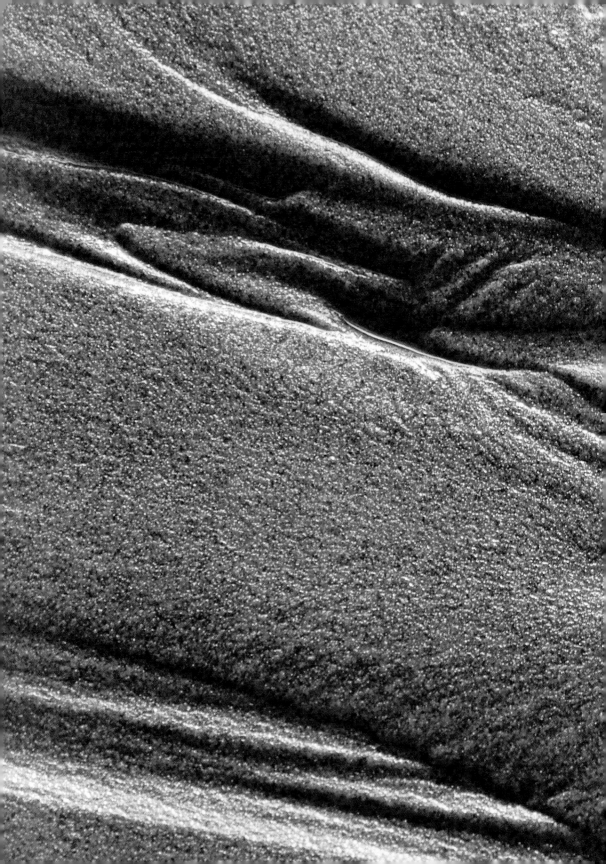

The Midas Myth of Goldfinger

THE MYTH: In the 1964 movie *Goldfinger*, Shirley Eaton played the part of Jill Masterson, a secretary to the evil Bond villain Auric Goldfinger. After she betrayed Goldfinger, she was murdered by having her skin painted gold. Ever since, the myth has endured: If you paint your entire body with gold paint, you can easily die because your skin won't be able to breathe. Another part of the myth was the possible solution: Leave a small, unpainted patch of skin at the base of your spine and you'll be safe.

HISTORICAL NOTE

 During Elizabethan times, lead was an essential ingredient in theater makeup. Many actors died from lead poisoning, a slow and painful process.

PETER: "Normally she would not have done such an interview, but she was intrigued. We did the initial experiment first, then I went to England with a crew and did a separate shoot. We spent a couple of hours with her in a hotel room and talked through the whole thing. One thing that's not generally known is that they left her entire chest unpainted, not the base of the spine. In the scene, they only painted the parts of her that were visible to the camera. Plus, they didn't use paint, they used makeup. Even though they used makeup on her that they knew would breathe, they left her entire front unpainted in deference to the myth."

THE PLAN: Paint Jamie with gold latex paint (as opposed to oil-based or enamel paint).

PETER: "We used latex paint because of its nonbreathability, which is what oil-based gold paint is supposed to be."

To test the myth, before being painted Jamie ran on a treadmill for ten minutes while his vital signs were measured. Prior to the workout, his heart rate was measured at 136 and his body temperature was 96.8 degrees. After the brief workout, Jamie's blood oxygen was measured at 80 percent, while his body temperature rose to 97.8 degrees, all perfectly normal.

Also, before completely painting Jamie's body, a test patch was first painted on to ensure that the gold powder used for the paint color wouldn't cause any complications. Then, after shaving his body and applying two coats of latex paint (which doesn't allow skin to breathe or sweat), Jamie was urged to drink a lot of water to avoid dehydration.

The process continued with a third coat of gold paint while the MythBusters constantly monitored Jamie's vital signs during the whole time he was painted. Since both Jamie and Adam were skeptical that leaving a small, unpainted patch at the base of the spine would eliminate any danger, an EMT team was standing by. Since there had been no ill effects from the test patch, the small of Jamie's back was painted over as well, in flagrant disregard to the Goldfinger myth. After the painting was finished, he jogged on the treadmill again to see if there was a change.

Jamie didn't anticipate having any problems from being painted gold. However, his blood pressure was elevated, which immediately worried the medics. Jamie began to feel flulike symptoms, chills, and hot flashes. The experiment was called off when these strange symptoms persisted. The removal of the latex paint was just as strange.

JAMIE: "It felt like I was being skinned."

Stripped of his painted skin, Jamie quickly recuperated. Still, his reactions to the latex paint remained a mystery.

As a result of Jamie's strange reaction to the paint, the myth would eventually be "revisited."

Myth Revisited: Adam goes for the Midas touch

In the original experiment, Jamie showed some anomalous readings that nobody understood, so it was decided that when the MythBusters revisited the myth, Adam would be the next "golden boy" to get latexed. The experiment was repeated with one small difference. While Jamie's core temperature was measured with an ear probe, it wasn't deemed accurate enough. Adam's core temperature was best taken with a rectal temperature probe. Ouch.

Like Jamie, Adam shaved his entire body. Medics measured his heart rate, blood pressure, and core temperature.

Before his paint job, Adam's temperature was 99 degrees. His blood pressure was 120 over 80, and his heart rate was 57 and relaxed. The latex paint was mixed with a pigment and was allowed to dry gold and sticky. And just to be on the safe side, Adam was left with some bare, unpainted skin.

After an hour of being painted gold, Adam's heart rate and blood pressure didn't move. His core body temperature, taken anally and accurately, dropped to 97.5, as opposed to rising. His other vital signs were fine too. After Adam's golden days were over, it was concluded that Jamie's elevated blood pressure during the first experiment was probably due to his personal physiology and probably not related to the gold paint at all.

JAMIE: "The paint felt very strange."

ADAM: "It was really awful. Both Jamie and I felt hot and cold, you can't quite describe it, that tightness just before you get sick. But it's all over your body. I wore that paint for ninety minutes."

PETER: "Once they were painted, both Jamie's and Adam's demeanors totally changed."

MYTH STATUS: STILL BUSTED

Jamie's strange symptoms aside, the Goldfinger myth was roundly busted twice and safely put to bed.

SCIENTIFIC PRINCIPLE

PETER: "The science of the experiment deals with the respiration of the human body and the transformation of air between skin, and the concept that it's not as significant in terms of respiration because most of our air obviously comes from breathing through our lungs."

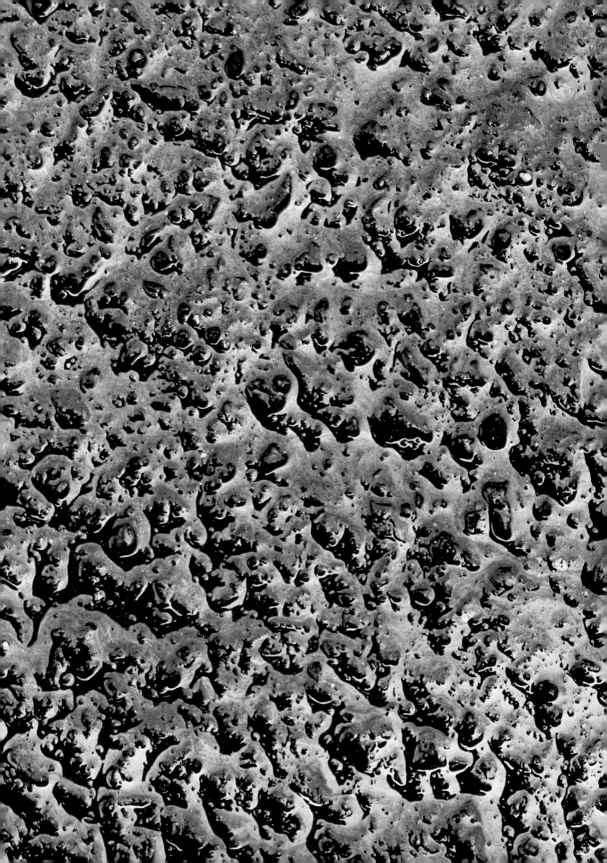

Can a 1967 Chevy Impala mounted with a rocket booster make it to 350 mph?

Jet–Assisted Chevy or JATO Car

THE MYTH: A former Air Force sergeant mounted a military JATO—or Jet-Assisted Takeoff—rocket on a 1967 Chevy Impala out in the Arizona desert. He made sure he had a long straight road and that there was nothing around. Then, when he got up to highway speed at about 80 mph, he fired the JATO off. The car accelerated from 80 to 300 mph in seconds. Unfortunately, there was a curve in the road, a slight upgrade, and a mountain shortly thereafter. He applied the brakes, which of course burned out. He left about a mile and a half of skid marks. He didn't make the turn. He went airborne approximately 100 or so feet up in the air and crashed into the side of the mountain. The highway patrol found smoldering wreckage.

THE PLAN: Since there hadn't been any corroborating evidence to support this modern legend, the most obvious starting point for the MythBusters in putting this myth to the test was to locate a 1967 Chevy Impala that could still run, and then persuade the United States Air Force to furnish them with either a JATO or a RATO (Rocket-Assisted Takeoff). Since it's illegal for civilians to own a JATO, it was necessary to enlist the military to help supervise the MythBusters' Jet-Assisted Chevy experiment. After scouring the Bay Area and checking out various American-made cars from the late 1960s,

Adam and Jamie located a working 1966 Chevy Impala, complete with raked-up remote control hydraulic shock absorbers. However, the military categorically denied the MythBusters' request to provide them with any JATO or RATO units.

JAMIE: "Jet-Assisted Takeoff technology has been around since the Second World War. Technically, they should be called RATOs, because each canister is filled with solid rocket propellant. A single unit exerts a thousand pounds of thrust for twelve to fifteen seconds. Up to eight JATOs are used when large military

aircraft operate with heavy loads or take off from short runways. Since one pound of thrust is two horsepower, each JATO tank will give off a total of two thousand horsepower of additional get-up-and-go."

After the military nixed access to a JATO unit, Jamie proceeded with Plan B, which was to secure the use of hobby rocket tubes.

JAMIE: "The upper-end classes of hobby rockets are actually more powerful than some JATOs, and they're smaller, which made it easier to mount them up on the roof of the Impala. But while they put out fifteen hundred pounds of thrust instead of a thousand, the propulsion lasts only four seconds instead of twelve to fifteen seconds."

ADAM: "The plan was to mount three of them stacked on top of each other on a reinforced Impala roof and set them off successively. Because a federal license is needed to purchase them and set them off, Jamie found a qualified operator who agreed to fire off the hobby rockets at the site. Since each rocket represents fifteen hundred pounds of thrust and three thousand horsepower, our Chevy junker would be almost four times as powerful as an Indy car."

JAMIE: "The Chevrolet Impala was the ideal candidate for urban legend status. First introduced in 1958, it was a prestige car within the means of the average American. By the end of the millennium, sales exceeded thirteen million, making the Impala the most popular full-sized car in American history."

Before sending the '66 Chevy out to certain destruction,

Adam and Jamie gutted the inside of the car, chucked the seats, and reinforced the roof at eight points in order to mount the tubing rack to hold the three hobby rockets in place.

Since driving such a death machine on the open desert would be ill advised, Jamie rigged up the 3,000-pound projectile to be radio controlled. But the radio control had dangerous limitations.

JAMIE: "Since the control transmitter was only good for a thousand meters or a half mile, the car could potentially reach three hundred miles per hour and zoom out of range quickly."

Fail-safe mechanisms were installed in the radio control unit to kick in and control the car should Jamie lose communication with the vehicle. The plan was to engage the car by remote control to a speed of 80 mph. Then, with Jamie and the rocketry expert flying above in a helicopter, they would set off the three jet rockets.

After locating a flat, dry lakebed between San Francisco and Los Angeles, the Jet-Assisted Chevy myth was ready to be put to the test once and for all.

THE EXPERIMENT:

A rocket science expert on site warned that Adam and Jamie's jet-powered Chevy experiment could be doomed from the start.

ADAM: "The hobby rockets, he warned, weren't fastened down strong enough, nor were they installed straight, which could result in the car being unable to steer straight ahead. Wind resistance would be the biggest problem.

Theoretically, if a standard Impala takes off at three hundred fifty miles and hour, the sheer force of the velocity would blow out its windows and pull the roof off. Plus, the air currents would raise the front end upward, causing the car to go airborne and flip over."

But the MythBusters' raked-out Impala was anything but standard. With its automatic hydraulic shocks, the lower-than-usual front end would give the car considerable aerodynamic efficiency.

After a dry run, all remote systems were go. But once the helicopter was up and running for the first launch, the car engine died. It was only a minor

setback, though. After the Impala's fuel filter was flushed out and cleaned of sediments, the engine was restored to running order.

On the second try, as the helicopter approached the Chevy, the Impala's brakes were released. It began to move forward. Within minutes, the car reached the magic speed of 80 mph. On cue, the three rockets were fired seconds apart. The car shot forward brilliantly with unbridled, hell-raising speed. The MythBusters had a liftoff.

Every three seconds, another 1,000 pounds of thrust were added to the Chevy, as if it were powered by a JATO. Fifteen-foot flames shot out the back of each rocket.

THE RESULT:

JAMIE: "The Jet-Assisted Chevy took off like a shot. The car did not go end over end. The body did not self-destruct or go airborne, as the experts had predicted. In fact, the car zoomed so fast, the helicopter pilot struggled to keep pace with the rocket-charged Impala—and a chopper's top speed is as high as a hundred and thirty miles an hour!"

The Jet-Assisted Chevy adventure was one of the most thrilling moments in Jamie's professional special effects career.

JAMIE: "It was hysterical, absolutely outrageous. Once those rockets lit, the car shot off horizontally. It was a lot of fun, those few seconds being in the chopper trailing behind the car and seeing those rockets set off. It was indescribable."

MYTH STATUS: BUSTED

The Impala experiment went off spectacularly. But did it replicate the myth?

ADAM: "Given the structure of the original myth, that the guy ignited the rocket and accelerated to three hundred fifty miles an hour, then hit the edge of the curve of the road and was airborne for several seconds before hitting the side of the cliff, do you think it's possible?"

JAMIE: "Didn't happen. To reach three hundred fifty miles an hour, you would have to have had at least four times the power that we did."

Incidentally, when asked about the myth of the Jet-Assisted Chevy, the Arizona Department of Public Safety says that there is no record such an accident occurred. While it was quite a grand experiment out on the lakebed, the MythBusters, in actual fact, busted the myth as being improbable. Myth busted!

JAMIE: "This was my favorite experiment. The JATO rocket car was cool because it represented the most extravagant type of urban legend and one of the most spectacularly stupid and dangerous things that people often do. What more can you do than strap a JATO rocket on top of your car and set it off? It was imaginative and over the top. The image of setting it off was spectacular with that beautiful roar. It was as beautiful as watching a jaguar run across the plains of Africa. While it may not have had as much sociological interest or redeeming social value as some of the others, for me, it was just fun."

SCIENTIFIC PRINCIPLE

PETER: "*Power-to-weight ratio.* Jamie and Adam had to do quite a lot of calculations about what kind of thrusts we'd get from the rockets, and for how long, and how that would convert to horsepower, and what that meant in terms of moving an object that weighs four thousand pounds.

"*Air resistance on the car.* Race car driver Andy Granatelli said that even if you had the power to get a car up to speed, it would never do three hundred fifty miles an hour. He felt you'd be lucky to get a Chevy Impala over two hundred miles per hour without the car either being torn to pieces or flipping and crashing.

"*Aerodynamics.* There was some speculation that the car at that speed would behave like a wing and become airborne after it created its own lift. Anticipating that, we jacked up the rear end, thinking it would hold it down on the ground."

Can a scuba diver be sucked up by a firefighting helicopter, flown over a forest fire, and dropped into the middle of the flames?

The Scuba Diver Forest Fire Myth

THE MYTH: The well-known story goes that a scuba diver was found in a tree in the middle of a charred forest about 50 miles inland. Speculation was that the scuba diver was scooped up by a firefighting helicopter or airplane and dumped into the flaming forest. This story has been around since at least 1987, circulating in California, Australia, British Columbia, and France. It has showed up in TV episodes and films. But is it plausible?

PETER: "The reason it was so important to do the myth was because it was such a prominent one. Of course, everyone knew about this one."

THE PLAN: The MythBusters' first course of action was to research water-gathering planes and helicopters used for firefighting to see if such a scenario was remotely possible. Since the 1940s, firefighters have used water dropped from aircraft to help control forest fires. Some fixed-wing aircraft skim water from the surfaces of lakes and oceans. But the biggest water bomber in the world had an intake scoop that was only 6 inches in diameter, far too small to fit a scuba diver.

The myth was still conceivably possible with a helicopter, though, and one of the most popular helicopter water drop systems is much like an upside-down parachute with a hole in the center. It's dropped from a helicopter and lowered into the water, and as the helicopter rises, the bucket fills with water. Once the helicopter arrives at the drop location, the pilot pulls a cable and a valve is released that dumps 120 gallons of water onto the fire. All of these helicopters are equipped with mirrors, so theoretically, the pilot would be able to see a living thing struggling in the bucket. More significant, however, is the bucket's size.

ADAM: "There's no way a scuba diver could fit into a bucket. It's far too small and has dozens of straps—like a parachute. That part of the myth was busted out of the gate."

But Jamie discovered a third system, called the Erickson sky crane, a huge 10-ton helicopter tanker with a hose coming down out of the tank. A pump on the end of the hose sucks in water at the rate of 2,000 gallons per minute.

Could there be enough suction generated at the end of that hose to suck up a diver by the torso, pick him up, and carry him for miles out of the water?

ADAM: "No one would let us near one while it was running. The pump itself cost around thirty thousand dollars. We couldn't rent one. No one wanted to demo a helicopter for us. It became totally impossible. Finally, Peter said we had to build it, to take something like an outboard motor and extend it or something. Jamie and I were both skeptical about the feasibility of doing that."

THE EXPERIMENT: What makes a sky crane's pump suck is a propeller blade, like that on the end of a standard outboard motor. So the MythBusters decided to obtain an outboard motor, and with a little welding, reorient the direction of the propellers so that the motor would operate as a pump. They discovered that a secondhand outboard rated at 225 horsepower and run at half-throttle could function the same as (or better than) the pump installed on the end of an Erickson heli-tanker.

JAMIE: "I don't remember Peter coming up with the outboard motor idea. Did he?"

ADAM: "Peter did come up with the idea to use the outboard motor, because I was specifically thinking it was a stupid idea when I first heard it. And yet, forced to do it, Jamie and I muscled through it, and in the end, our pump exceeded the real pump's stats by thirty percent. That was very satisfying."

A frame for the outboard was welded together. Then the original outboard driveshaft was removed. The MythBusters built a new and much longer driveshaft. Because it spun at a high revolutions per minute (rpm), the shaft was accurately machined on the lathe and the propellers were cut down and carefully balanced to avoid excessive vibration. The propeller was then adjusted to run the wrong way around, so that rather than pushing water down, it sucked water up, toward the outboard. To control the water flow, the shaft was encased in a heavy steel pipe with a 10-inch inside diameter. A torrent of water sucked up by the outboard was vented away from the motor by angling the pipe. Finally, the entire contraption was painted fire engine red. Mounted on a forklift and weighing close to half a ton, the MythBusters' scuba-sucking rig would attempt to suck up a submerged Buster dressed in a wet suit.

Adam and Jamie tested the pump out on Buster the dummy using a high school swimming pool. But first the MythBusters had to meet their water-sucking-capacity goal of extracting 3,000 gallons a minute. A large 2,000-gallon tank was set next to the rig, and a 10-inch-diameter hose was fitted to the pump and put into the pool. Then the 10-inch-diameter pipe was tied to the measuring tank. The MythBusters' homemade outboard motor pump would have to fill the 2,000-gallon tank in at least 45 seconds. The initial test run proved successful: The tank was filled in well under 30 seconds. The MythBusters' rig sucked big time!

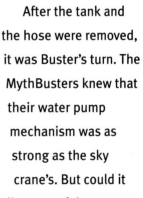

After the tank and the hose were removed, it was Buster's turn. The MythBusters knew that their water pump mechanism was as strong as the sky crane's. But could it suck a scuba diver out of the water and hold him in the air long enough to arrive at a forest fire?

THE RESULT: The noisy underwater pump, equipped with a funnel and fish guard, failed to suck Buster in. In an attempt to increase the suction, the MythBusters removed the funnel and guard.

ADAM: "During that test Buster was held fast underwater by the pump's suction, but as soon as he broke the surface and the pump sucked air, he was freed. Without the pressure of the water, the pump's motor would have over-revved and disintegrated. Buster broke free each time the sucking hose left the water."

MYTH STATUS:

JAMIE: "There was no way the suction would maintain long enough to carry a diver out of the water and inland to a forest fire. While the pump did pull Buster out of the water, it was only a few inches. As Adam reminded us, 'A little bit is far short of a trip to a forest fire.' Since the pump needed to be continuously primed with water in order to hold the weight of a diver, that ended the scuba diver myth. It was undeniably busted."

SCIENTIFIC PRINCIPLE

PETER: "Scientifically, this myth dealt with what you need to create suction and how a pump works. Before working on *MythBusters*, I didn't know that pumps needed to be primed. On top of that, Adam and Jamie's machine had to be *self*-priming because the mechanism had to drop into the water; otherwise, it wouldn't have worked. What that meant was that as soon as it broke the surface, there was no more suction."

The ultimate roach revenge, or another excuse for the *MythBusters* crew to blow things up?

Bug Bomb!

THE MYTH: A family in a 500-square-foot house had a bug problem and decided to take care of it with aerosol bug bombs. Unfortunately, they used *twelve* bug bombs, though one bomb could easily handle a 700-square-foot house. When they left the house to wait out the bug killing, they heard a loud boom. Bug Bomb! Their entire house had been blown to smithereens by the pesticides igniting and setting fire to the house.

THE PLAN: Adam and Jamie got things started by setting up a miniature Plexiglas house to test the explosive qualities of bug bombs. Since the myth didn't specify what household appliance had sparked the explosion that ignited the fogger gas, they tested several possible household culprits. Adam designed an igniter panel with four different types of ignition sources: a pilot light operation; a standard wall plug device with faulty wiring; a house thermostat that emitted a tiny spark; and a stove igniter that created a continuous spark. All the igniters were wired back to a single control box that could be set off remotely. After throwing the faulty wiring switch, they managed to blow up the mini-model plastic box with one fogger inside. The MythBusters had succeeded in turning a fogger into an incendiary device. For their next trick, they needed a real house to send into orbit.

THE EXPERIMENT: In order to solve the Bug Bomb myth, Adam and Jamie and the MythBusters team located a house already earmarked for demolition. Inside the vacant dwelling, they sealed off the hallway and all the extra rooms in order to bring the area down to the original 500 square feet. Flammable carpets were removed, and a rope was attached to an unlocked sliding glass door so they could ventilate the house in case the bug spray didn't explode.

ADAM: "Next it was time to drop the bomb . . . or twelve. The crew set off twelve bug bombs inside the house, more than ten times the

manufacturer's recommended amount. The air was thick and toxic. Even with gas masks, the crew needed to get out fast. As the house filled with fogger fumes, the team took its positions behind the blast screen two hundred feet away."

Adam fired up each of the ignition systems by remote. The result? No bug bomb blast.

PETER: "We tend to pump the flammable stuff in there, hoping it will get a huge explosion, and the reality is that you should actually do the opposite. Just have a naked flame in there and gradually increase the concentrations until you get just the right air-fuel mixtures and—poof!—there it goes. The problem with that, of course, is that it tends to explode at a much lower level, so you don't get the big result that we were expecting."

Although the stove igniter functioned properly with a visible open flame, there was still no explosion. As the air cleared, the MythBusters were mystified. After all, things had blown up just fine back at the workshop.

JAMIE: "Blowing up a house with bug bombs is not quite as easy as we thought. It's not that it's difficult, it's just they need very specific conditions regarding fuel mixtures."

To do that, they installed a much bigger flame igniter and set off far more bug bombs than was safe or sane. The result was one huge blast, enough for the entire house to explode and blow out a main window.

ADAM: "Here on *MythBusters Makeover*, we turned this lovely California bungalow into a disaster zone."

THE RESULT:

Bug bombs can become real firebombs because they're highly flammable. The propellant in many aerosol bug bombs has a petroleum or propane base that does indeed burn under the right conditions.

PETER: "Exploding House was another one where we knew the myth was true. There were reports of using too many bug bombs and blowing houses off their foundations. The question was how to do it. Sometimes we have incredible difficulty getting things to blow up. Igniting things can be a big deal for us. It took us three days to actually show scientifically that gasoline can light with the proper mix. Sometimes it's actually quite hard to make flammables ignite."

MYTH STATUS: CONFIRMED

JAMIE: "It's definitely confirmed. We blew the doors out. We had to do a little fussing around with the ignition source, but it's true. It will happen."

ADAM: "Bug bombs plus ignition source equals boom! No doubt the myth is confirmed."

SCIENTIFIC PRINCIPLE

PETER: "It has to do with air fuel mixtures. It's another classic case where we have to do stuff in preliminary testing before we go to full scale. We've also tested flour and sawdust air fuel mixtures that explode in silos. We've recreated a flour and air fuel explosion, and only a small sawdust and air fuel one. The other finding of a science nature with the Bug Bomb experiment is that with the multiple ignition sources we use it's difficult to get an electrical spark to ignite anything. We'll have four or five ignition sources, including a stove sparker, and we usually end up having to use regular matches. With sparking electrical power points, for example, you have to have the fuel and air mixture absolutely perfect. Also, the air temperature and the humidity have to be exact."

SAFETY NOTE

Turn off all ignition sources, open flames, pilot lights, running electrical appliances, and thermostats before using bug bombs. Always read the label, and don't try this at home. According to the Environmental Protection Agency, it certainly is no myth. "It occurs in California at least once or twice per year," said Paul H. Gosselin of the Department of Pesticide Regulation. "People overload the number of these foggers in their dwelling to the point where it fills up and they forget to shut off their pilot light or other ignition source and blow out windows and to some extent, can blow up and destroy the entire structure."

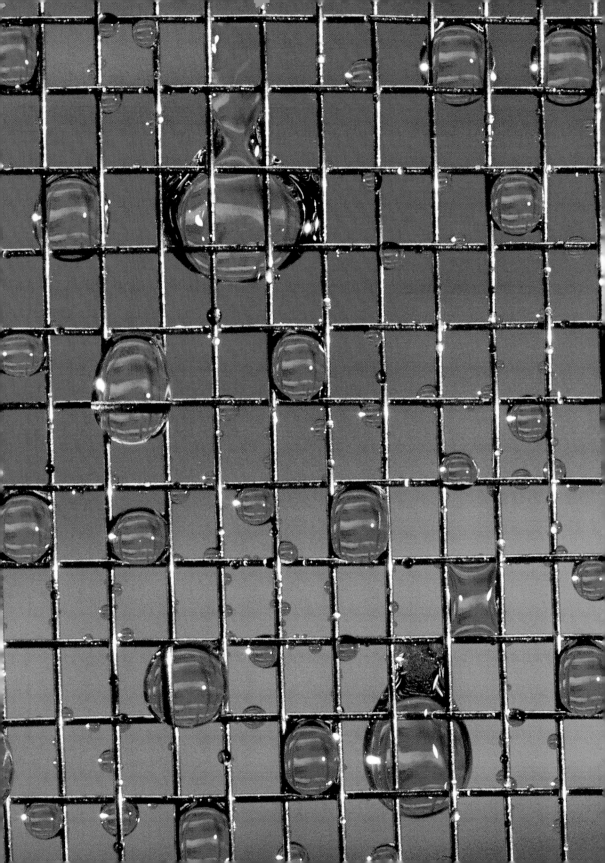

Adam and Jamie plunge to new depths when they try to salvage a submerged sailboat in the silliest fashion. Can you really raise a sunken boat to the surface by filling it with Ping-Pong balls?

Ping-Pong Salvage, or How Many Ping-Pong Balls Does It Take to Float Your Boat?

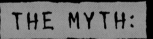

THE MYTH: Can you raise a ship from the bottom of the sea using thousands and thousands of Ping-Pong balls?

In a 1940s Donald Duck comic book, Donald's nephews, Huey, Dewey, and Louie, had the comical idea to raise a sunken boat using Ping-Pong balls. Silly idea? Salvage companies frequently use large air-filled flotation bags to raise boats off the ocean floor. In 1998 a slightly different technique was used to raise a piece of the *Titanic*'s historic hull. It took five giant bags—each filled with 6,000 gallons of lightweight propane—to lift the giant 20-ton piece. Was the ducks' idea comical, plausible, or both?

THE PLAN:

To prepare for their experiment, the MythBusters needed to answer some questions.

Q: *How would a Ping-Pong ball hold up underwater? Would it be subject to pressure, and crack?*

A: The MythBusters found out by simulating conditions inside a pressurized chamber that a Ping-Pong ball under 60 psi of pressure, at approximately 90 feet underwater, would not crack. Therefore, pressure would not be a factor in the experiment.

Q: *How much space does a whole bunch of Ping-Pong balls occupy?*

A: Ping-Pong balls have only a 51 percent packing efficiency, meaning they don't stack together very economically.

Q: *How many Ping-Pong balls does it take to lift 1 pound underwater?*

A: Adam's calculation revealed that fifteen Ping-Pong balls could offset 1 pound of weight underwater.

The MythBusters' search for a boat to sink ended with the discovery of a retired fiberglass sailboat named the *Jalapeno*. Using Adam's calculations, the small 25-foot vessel, weighing in at about 3,500 pounds, would take just over 50,000 Ping-Pong balls to make neutrally buoyant. A total of 60,000 balls could raise it from the bottom of the ocean to the surface. Fortunately, the boat had enough nooks and crannies to fit the necessary number of balls.

PETER: "Our skilled researcher got us Ping-Pong balls for free that had been used for avalanche research in Japan. Plus, they were multicolored."

How would the MythBusters get 60,000 Ping-Pong balls down to the bottom of the sea in order to raise a sunken boat?

PETER: "We had no idea how we were going to get those balls down into the boat. We thought of all kinds of stuff. Little hands that could grab the Ping-Pong balls and take them down on conveyor belts. I was looking for something involved, something to give the story some meat. We could have gone down with bags, put the balls inside and filled up the boat, and lifted it up in five seconds. But I thought we needed to do something spectacular. Then Jamie comes up with this idea, which was that you could pour water down into the ocean, and because Ping-Pong balls float, they will go down with the water into the ocean, which to Adam and me was totally, completely, and utterly counterintuitive."

JAMIE: "Why not see if a flow of water downward would carry the Ping-Pong balls down with it? As gravity takes the water down, maybe it will pull the Ping-Pong balls down with it."

Sure enough, Jamie was correct. So, using a giant funnel and a long piece of tubing, then simply adding gravity, water, and Ping-Pong balls, the MythBusters were able to devise a system that could efficiently flush thousands of Ping-Pong balls down into a sunken boat.

PETER: "Jamie's rig was an absolutely brilliant piece of design. That experiment was the essence of what Jamie's best at, the incredibly simple mechanical solution. I've even had engineers marvel at it."

The doomed vessel was towed to Monterey Bay and prepared for sinking. The *Jalapeno,* rechristened *Mythtanic II,* was flooded with water. (As she sank, Adam boarded the craft in order to re-bust the original *Mythtanic* myth about sinking ships creating a deadly vortex while plummeting. Once again, Adam did not go down with the ship. There was no vortex. That myth remained busted.)

THE EXPERIMENT:

As a truckload of 60,000 Ping-Pong balls pulled up to Monterey Bay, the MythBusters discussed the dangers of the experiment.

JAMIE: "Working inside of a sunken vessel, the divers had to be careful of their air consumption rates and watch out for any dramatic losses in buoyancy. If a hatch cover blew, causing thousands of Ping-Pong balls to dramatically escape, that might cause the vessel to dangerously sink back down.

Caution was also taken in protecting the local wildlife from swallowing any stray Ping-Pong balls."

After sealing off the salvage area in order to keep marine life safe and separate, the experiment began. While Adam fed the balls into the rig above the surface, Jamie was down below, underwater, marshalling balls into *Mythtanic II.*

ADAM: "After only a few minor setbacks and adjustments, the rig worked beautifully, as an estimated fifty thousand Ping-Pong balls were ready to be poured into *Mythtanic II.* But by the halfway mark, right around twenty-five thousand balls, *Mythtanic II* had already taken in enough Ping-Pong balls to become buoyantly neutral."

A few questions remained.

ADAM: "Was the sunken ship's deck strong enough to lift the boat's eighteen-hundred-pound keel from the mud? Would the deck rip apart, causing thirty thousand Ping-Pong balls to flood Monterey Bay?"

Fortunately, neither was the case.

THE RESULT: After only a minor rupture, which was quickly repaired, *Mythtanic II* withstood Ping-Pong pressure and slowly broke the water's surface. After a nine-hour MythBusting marathon, the Ping-Pong salvage was officially and successfully over. Official Ping-Pong count needed to surface *Mythtanic II*: 27,000 balls.

MYTH STATUS: PLAUSIBLE

The MythBusters originally calculated that it would take at least 60,000 Ping-Pong balls to raise *Mythtanic II*. But because of the sailboat's wood and fiberglass construction, factors Adam and Jamie hadn't taken into account, only about half that amount was needed. Also, Jamie's Ping-Pong pump principle, a method inspired by a comic book seventy years ago, worked like a charm.

JAMIE: "Sometimes the simplest solution can be quite elegant. There is an interesting dynamic between the three of us, where I might have a clear vision while Peter's got visual concerns that he has to throw into the mix, and while Adam is this headlong stream of energy in addition to being quite adept and knowledgeable in a lot of the same fields as I am. All of this interacts into what makes the show what it is."

Microwave Madness

The humble microwave oven. Is it a modern, handy dandy cooking device . . . or a mysterious machine with dark and frightening powers?

THE MYTH: Microwave ovens are magnets for urban legends. Here, the MythBusters put some of the main ones to the test.

SCIENTIFIC PRINCIPLE

How do microwaves work?

PETER: "A microwave oven uses radio waves to cook food. A device called a magnetron bombards the inside of the oven with radio waves, which react with the water molecules in the food, causing them to vibrate at an enormous speed. That friction creates heat, which cooks the food. In the early days, the microwave oven was hailed as a revolutionary kitchen convenience. Today the average home microwave oven is rated at eleven hundred watts."

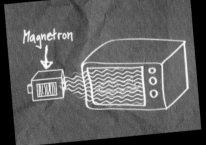

Magnetron

MICROWAVE MYTH #1: Broiled Again

Can a tanning bed cook your innards?

While 30 million Americans tan indoors at tanning salons, one microwave myth has caught on and spread like tanning lotion. Can a tanning machine microwave the innards of a human being? Many different versions of this story sprout regularly.

Will overexposure result in baked intestines? Jamie and Adam, not the tanning bed types, elected to let a couple of raw chickens take the risk.

ADAM: "After giving the birds four straight forty-eight-minute sessions on a tanning bed underneath the hot lights, while the birds sported an outward burn, no noticeable cooking occurred on the inside."

Warning: Please don't try this at your local tanning salon. That many sessions in a row would result in serious sunburn.

So, do tanning beds put out microwaves?

ADAM: "Absolutely not! Tanning beds put out light waves. Plus, contrary to popular misconception, microwaves don't cook from the inside out. Microwaves heat from the outside in."

FINAL VERDICT BUSTED

MICROWAVE MYTH #2: Microwaved Metal

Can microwaving metal make your oven explode? Is a spoon in a coffee cup inside a microwave oven a sign of sudden death?

ADAM: "I once had a roommate who made me buy him a new microwave because I put a spoon inside it."

Adam and Jamie microwaved several metal objects. Just to be safe, they watched the results from behind a lexan shield, a bulletproof material used in the windshields of NASCARs.

ADAM: "The first metallic subject we tried was a teaspoon, which resulted in the spoon getting really, really hot. But that was it. No arcing or buzzing. A fork performed the same way. No sparks flew."

JAMIE: "Tin foil scrunched into a ball had an unusual visual effect. The microwave caused an electric charge to build up in the metal while scrunching or folding the foil allowed the charge to jump the gaps, creating a mini light show; spectacular, yes, but not explosive."

Warning: Microwaving metal might result in magnetron meltdown.

FINAL VERDICT BUSTED
(WITH THE FOLLOWING PROVISION)

If microwaved metal contacts the sides of the oven, arcing can occur that could feed back into the magnetron, which could reduce its lifespan.

ADAM: "A good friend of mine who is a science geek called me after that one and said, 'You improved my quality of life. Once I discovered I could put tin foil in the microwave without its being close to the side, I now heat my burritos with a little bit of tin foil on the end thirty percent and it cooks the whole thing perfectly!'"

MICROWAVE MYTH #3: Exploding Water

If you overheat water in a microwave, and you take the cup out of the oven, can the water explode in your face, injuring or burning you?

PETER: "Tap water always boils because it has impurities. Distilled water has no impurities, meaning no boil."

After a little research, Adam and Jamie found out that the only way water could explode is if it's superheated beyond its boiling point without actually

boiling. So the MythBusters put two cups of water together in the microwave, one distilled, one tap. When the tap water boiled, they knew that the distilled water had become superheated. Then, dropping an impurity like a sugar cube into the distilled water made the boiling process happen instantly and violently. The MythBusters created exploding water.

ADAM: "Don't try this at home. If someone were holding the cup, they would definitely be severely burned."

PETER: "This was another totally infuriating experiment because apart from seeing the foil arc, some of the results—like the exploding water—were extremely difficult to reproduce until we understood how to do it. It's an example of a result where, yes it can happen, but the circumstances have to be very specific."

FINAL VERDICT CONFIRMED AND TRUE

Can the MythBusters use modern technology to tackle a centuries-old cliché?

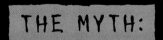

Needle in the Haystack

Is it possible to find a needle in a haystack? And if so, how long would it take?

THE PLAN: To test out this famous old adage, the two city boys drove a truck out to the country to visit a hay farm, where they loaded up on twenty bales of hay. Then they stopped off at a sewing supply store to pick up two sets of various-sized needles, which they planned to hide inside the hay.

ADAM: "Back when the saying first took stock, most sewing needles were made out of bone, so to make the experiment a little tougher, and in keeping with the tradition of the myth, a bone needle was included in the search. That meant we needed to devise a modern technique of separating the needles beyond ordinary magnetic or metal-detecting methods."

PETER: "Sometimes there's not much in the way of science with these old wives' tales, but it's fun to see the way Jamie and Adam come up with their separate solutions. There's always that difficulty getting the right mix between scientific principle and entertainment."

THE EXPERIMENT: The MythBusters divided into two teams and developed two competing systems to conduct the experiment. The object was for each team to sort through ten bales (roughly 1,000 pounds of hay) and find three various-sized metallic needles and one larger bone needle within the mass.

Whose machine would find all four needles first?

JAMIE: "I figured the easiest way to find a needle in the haystack was to burn down the haystack. I designed my machine, Dante's Inferno, to separate out the needles and burn the rest. Hay was blown through a rotating ten-foot PVC tubing with slots cut in it so that the needles might be able to fall through. Magnets were also set up at the end of the tube to catch any that made it to the end. Then, as a fail-safe process, a leaf blower motor transferred the hay into a steel drum furnace unit, which would burn everything but metal and bone."

ADAM: "My approach was markedly different. I constructed a shallow waterproof tank with three agitator paddle wheels, dubbed the NeedleFinder 2000. Since hay floats and needles sink, after the hay went into the water and came out as sludge, the needles would, in theory, drop to the bottom of the tank. For my fail-safe approach, I added super-strong neodymium magnets to the front end of the feed trough to pick up any metal needles at the very beginning."

The MythBusters' ingenuity was on the line. Adam's team fed the hay along the water trough and out the other side, hoping the needles would sink to the bottom on the way through.

Jamie's hay was blown down the twisting tube, allowing the needles to separate and fall out the slots.

Who would win? Adam's paddle wheel NeedleFinder 2000 or Jamie's high-rotation Dante's Inferno slotted tube?

JAMIE: "After four hours, my team found the smallest metal needle first, which answered the age-old question of how long it takes to find a needle in the haystack. Well, four hours."

ADAM: "We both knew our machines were going to be effective when a few

minutes later my team located two metal needles stuck on the supermagnets."

After six hours, Adam found the third metal needle. With victory just a bone needle away, however, he admitted to a potential flaw. He had never checked to see if bone floats. It was a critical oversight, but with the race coming down to the wire, and after Jamie had found his second needle, Adam's bone needle was discovered.

The NeedleFinder 2000 had handily defeated Dante's Inferno.

MYTH STATUS: CONFIRMED

ADAM: "We proved conclusively that there are at least two unique ways to find a needle in a haystack, but it took a lot more time than expected. It was a total nightmare finding a needle in the haystack, and it really sucked sorting through a thousand pounds of wet hay."

JAMIE: "Adam did beat me fair and square, so I was actually happy for him."

ADAM: "The thing I liked about this episode was not the competitive aspect, but that it showed the totally different approaches we both used. Jamie and I do have very different ways to handle a problem and they can be equally successful, and that's interesting. Yeah, I won, but I probably won by only four or five minutes. As far as a contest over ten hours, we were both going to find all of those needles, no matter which method we were using."

SCIENTIFIC PRINCIPLE

PETER: "The only real bit of science in it was the fact that obviously a metal detector or a big magnet would have been the best way to go. What made it work was to put the bone needle in there, as if it were a contest two hundred years ago. Clearly it's still just as hard."

As far as science goes, does a bone needle float?

ADAM: "It's a minimal application of science, but more about the scientific aspect of sorting techniques. It represents diverse ways of thinking. You can watch Jamie and me approach it from two completely different ways—Jamie by fire and me by water."

JAMIE: "We both relied on gravity to sort it out. I took a long thin object and lined it up to where it would go through a slot because the tube was round and it was rolling and tossing, so the needles would get reoriented to where they could go through a small slot due to gravity. Adam used the water to accomplish the same means, but with less mechanical precision and more brute force. We both used magnets, but using brute force worked quicker. My machine was less able to handle an overload."

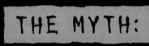

The MythBusters try to create a sinking feeling with quicksand. Not ordinary quicksand, but killer quicksand, the stuff that will suck you right under!

Killer Quicksand

THE MYTH: Does killer quicksand exist, the kind you see in Tarzan movies—the stuff that actually sucks you down and drowns you?

JAMIE: "This was an experiment I'd never really thought about before. Somewhere in the middle of it, it dawned on me: If saltwater makes you more buoyant, and sand and water get all mixed up, this is going to make you way more buoyant. There we were, up to our belly buttons, bobbing like corks."

The myth is not whether quicksand exists. People *have* gotten stuck in quicksand. The MythBusters set out to replicate killer quicksand that would create enough of a suction effect to drag someone all the way under, drowning them just like in the movies. It was another classic Hollywood horror image. Is there even a grain of truth to the killer quicksand story? Can someone *really* be sucked down into a bottomless pit?

Before they built their full-scale test apparatus, the MythBusters first needed to make a small-scale quicksand pit. After settling on two types of fine-

grained sand, Adam and Jamie had to figure out the density of their quicksand mix. If their quicksand was denser than normal water, it might be difficult to sink in it.

Quicksand is the result of a process called liquefaction. Water rises from under the ground, oversaturating sand or soil and reducing the friction between the particles until they can no longer bear any weight. In order to test the density of *their* quicksand, the MythBusters built a hydrometer, an instrument that measures a liquid's density.

Using 5-gallon buckets, a filtering device, and a garden hose, the MythBusters were able to see how different grains of sand behaved in relation to the water flow and filter. On a small scale, the MythBusters' quicksand looked potentially deadly. There was lots of suction. But while their miniature quicksand rig worked well, would they be able to create killer quicksand on a much grander level?

ADAM: "We found out that a bucket of sand weighs forty pounds, while a bucket of water and sand is a hundred and twenty pounds."

To perform the full-size experiment, the MythBusters used 20,000 pounds of sand, 15,000 pounds of water, and a big pump. They also enlisted a 2,000-gallon bucket. The 20,000 pounds of "sugar" sand arrived along with an engineering geologist. A diffuser was in place at the bottom of the tank to disperse the water upward through the sand, and once the water flowed at the right rate, the MythBusters ended up with 7 feet of quicksand.

But was it killer quicksand? Jamie had his doubts. Sand mixed with water makes water denser. Water with sand is heavier than water; hence, a body is bound to be more buoyant in quicksand than it would be in normal water.

ADAM: "The part of this show that I love the most is the opportunity to

operate large earth-moving machinery. Peter and I unabashedly love it. The most amazing thing is that you can pay a couple hundred bucks and some guy shows up with this giant tractor, hands you the keys, and drives away."

According to the geologist, the MythBusters had selected the perfect sand for the test. The fine-grained sand provided more surface area, so that when water flowed through it, the water would grab onto the sand and create the "quick" effect.

A MythBusters irrigation pump capable of circulating 14,000 gallons a minute created more than enough water flow. In fact, Adam and Jamie suddenly faced danger on two fronts. Could the guys be sucked under by killer quicksand? And, if the pump stopped during the experiment, could they die from being encased in 20,000 pounds of sand? Note: Don't try this at home.

THE EXPERIMENT:

The MythBusters' Killer Quicksand Rig was ready for testing. First the tank was filled with sand and water. Then the pump was turned on, adding hydration to the sand. Water was able to flow through the tank from the bottom while holding back the sand.

According to the hand-built hydrometer, the MythBusters quicksand was denser than water. The killer quicksand myth was on shaky ground. Nevertheless, a vine, a walking stick, and a metal bar that fit over the tank served as safety precautions, should Jamie and Adam begin to sink dangerously into killer quicksand.

After the pump had been switched on and the water began to rise through the sand, the liquefaction process occurred.

ADAM: "While inside the tank, I felt a sinking feeling, but once I sank to the middle of my chest in the sand and water mixture, I found my buoyancy point."

THE RESULT:

Adam's mass was far less dense than the quicksand, and as a result, he stayed suspended and very much alive. Jamie experienced the same buoyancy. He floated like a piece of Styrofoam.

MYTH STATUS:

While people and animals have certainly died in quicksand, Jamie concluded that they probably perished from exposure to the elements or dehydration. According to the results of the MythBusters' experiment, quicksand doesn't drag a victim slowly under and drown them.

JAMIE: "I noticed early in the experiment that you become quite buoyant since the quicksand is heavier than water, causing you to float like a cork."

The best thing to do if you're caught in quicksand is to lie on your back, bob around, and gently pull yourself out.

The final verdict on the Hollywood Killer Quicksand Myth:

ADAM: "Absolutely Busted. There is no such thing."

SCIENTIFIC PRINCIPLE

PETER: "The scientific principles involved here included buoyancy, specific density of materials, and liquefaction. The smaller the grain size, the quicker the sand is."

Is it possible to water-ski behind an eight-man rowing team?

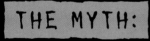

The Rowing Water Skier

THE MYTH: Can an eight-person rowing crew pull somebody up on water skis? Can a rowing craft and crew sustain the necessary power, human torque, and speed needed to ride the water on skis?

THE PLAN: Have Adam and Jamie created a brand-new outdoor sporting craze? It's called row skiing—skiing behind a rowboat. But can the strength and endurance of an eight-man rowing team pull it off? The MythBusters enlisted eight stalwart members of the Stanford University Varsity Rowing Team to see if it could be done.

ADAM: "We're going to ask eight strapping young lads in the prime of their life to yank us out of the water?"

JAMIE: "In this experiment, there was relatively little as far as 'the build,' but it was pretty involved. I had water-skied during my teens, but it had been a long time. When it came down to doing it, to make it work, I had to ignore all the instructions we were given and use both my arms and legs instead of just flexing my legs and keeping my back straight. I had to do what I had to do in order to absorb the shock."

PETER: "Waterskiing is usually performed at twenty miles per hour or more. In order to test this myth of human horsepower, eight charged college rowers with legs of steel and arms as strong as pipes would have to generate considerable acceleration fairly quickly. Even at top speeds, that's not taking into account the drag of the water-skier on the rowboat. It would be less daunting if Adam or Jamie each weighed a waiflike hundred pounds, but with Jamie tipping the scales between one hundred seventy and one hundred eighty pounds, the Stanford University rowers had a major task on their hands."

While there was no questioning the athletic prowess of the rowing team, neither Adam nor Jamie were avid water-skiers. After only a few lessons, Jamie learned to keep his arms straight, rise up slowly, keep his shoulders out, and stand tall—the perfect form of an accomplished water-skier. Thanks to his superior upper thigh and lower back strength, Jamie was to become the first MythBuster Varsity Ski Rower.

Would the rowing eight generate enough initial velocity? The lowest amount of speed required to pull Jamie up out of the water would be 10 mph. But at their fastest, during extreme competition, the Stanford rowers may generate a boat speed of 15 mph, again not counting Jamie's drag, which would slow them down.

THE EXPERIMENT:

The Stanford elite rowers showed up with a precision rowing craft made of sleek carbon fiber. Each of the two boats on site (one would help pace the other) was worth thousands of dollars. With an entire crew on board, each of the boats weighed nearly a ton in the water. Unlike the constant power from a conventional motorboat, once Jamie did get up on skis, in addition to navigating the lower speed, he had to absorb the many surges caused by each stroke of the rowing sequence.

ADAM: "Since the high-tech and somewhat fragile rowing shell didn't come standard with a towing hitch on the back, I needed to secure a towrope without ripping a hole in the boat. We accomplished this by running a line of thin, high-strength cord along both sides of the boat."

By distributing the load over the eight outriggers, Adam helped minimize the strain on the boat and its rowers.

THE RESULT: On his first attempt, Jamie managed to get up in the water on his skis. But he couldn't sustain the right posture.

JAMIE: "The tugging surges caused by the rowing momentum represented a real challenge."

In round two, it was already apparent that the Stanford rowers were capable of accelerating quickly enough. It was all down to Jamie being able to hold on. On his second attempt, Jamie managed to hold on for just a little longer, but still no cigar.

On his third and final try, Jamie was up and skiing.

ADAM: "Jamie held on and fought every bucking surge. Maneuvering his upper and lower body strength, he kept upright and skied for over forty seconds. For that short time period he water-skied like a champ, showing beyond a doubt that row skiing *could* be done."

Jamie and the Stanford rowing eight prevailed and proved that this weird myth was really possible.

JAMIE: "I was pleased that it worked. It went better than I had ever hoped. The fact that *I* could do this proves that it isn't as ridiculous as we thought. It was a real workout. I was breathing hard after all that trying to stay up."

SCIENTIFIC PRINCIPLE

JAMIE: "The science had to do with the size of the water ski as well as illustrating torque versus horsepower. We learned that eight really big guys could produce a lot of torque. At first I was worried about them getting me up out of the water, but I realized very quickly that once we did, it was more about keeping me out of the water and staying up because of the surges. That was the challenge. It was a purely physical stunt that required coordination, skill, and balance. But we went out and did it."

Can flying at high altitudes alter breast implants?

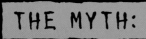

Exploding Implants!

THE MYTH: There once was a woman with silicone implants flying in an airplane on a short local flight inside a depressurized cabin. As the plane went higher, her implants got bigger and bigger and bigger until they finally exploded.

THE PLAN:

By estimation, well over 100,000 patients per year have some kind of cosmetic breast augmentation. Among patients who lead active lifestyles, a common worry is whether there's any danger to their implants if they fly in an airplane or skin-dive. The first step toward "exploding" the implant myth was to simulate a passenger by modifying a store dummy. Adam constructed a woman's torso made from ballistics gel that could house silicone implants.

ADAM: "The ballistics gel simulated skin, while the implants simulated, well, real implants. Since the gel was clear, it allowed us to observe any radical or subtle changes and movement of the implants inside the gelatin torso."

Next, the MythBusters converted a tank into a large chamber (equipped with vacuum and pressure pumps) that could reproduce the high altitude and low-pressure environment that allegedly caused the passenger's implants to expand and then explode.

JAMIE: "It was important to construct the large chamber as airtight as possible. As a result, some of the portholes were welded shut, while others were replaced. Afterward, an air pressure gauge was fitted onto the tank, which Adam calibrated, and then added an easy-to-read altitude guide."

THE EXPERIMENT: During the first round of experiments, the torso—with its implants—was placed inside the larger chamber and subjected to the typical in-flight cabin pressure conditions of roughly 8,000 feet above sea level. The only noticeable change to the implants were a few bubbles near the surface of the implant that grew larger, but certainly not large enough to expand the breast itself.

The big test came when the larger chamber matched the altitude of 35,000 feet, an impossible height for humans to fly in. Despite the lethal effects such high-altitude flying would have on the human body, the volume of the implants still appeared unchanged.

THE RESULT: JAMIE: "First, we observed the implants at about eight thousand feet. And after we bumped up [the altitude] to around thirty-five thousand feet, in both cases we saw only minimal expansion in the form of air bubbles, while the implants themselves showed no significant increase in volume."

Next, Jamie hooked up another, smaller chamber to emulate the high-pressure conditions of deep-sea diving. A single silicone implant inside the small chamber had no change at high pressure. Immediately after that, it was back to the larger chamber for another round of simulated high-altitude tests. In essence, the implants had taken a simulated trip from the bottom of the ocean floor to the highest summit of Everest. The MythBusters' experiment essentially replicated someone with implants diving into the water, then immediately getting onto a plane.

Once again, the MythBusters found no noticeable difference or effect on the implant.

Scientists at Duke University's Center for Hyperbaric Medicine have been studying the rigors of pressure on the human body for many years. They are aware of the concerns many people with implants have for their safety.

The findings of a series of plastic surgeons' studies concurred with the MythBusters. No change in altitude and pressure brought on any significant expansion of volume. Even if an implant were to double or triple in total volume, there was little or no danger that the outer shell would break, or in the case of the mythical passenger, explode.

MYTH STATUS: BUSTED

OR WAS IT?

The myth was truly, uh, busted (with no pun intended).

EXPLODING IMPLANTS REVISITED:

The Next Experiment

The sky-high drama of exploding implants continued as irate viewers challenged the MythBusters' findings. What about brassieres with inflatable air pockets in them? Could they have been the exploding inflatable culprits?

The MythBusters built a new chamber. A vacuum pump sucked out the air as an aircraft altimeter once again showed how much altitude was being simulated as "cabin" pressure dropped inside the new chamber. A blast screen protected the MythBusters from any unplanned undergarment implosions.

So the question remained, could an inflatable bra (as opposed to implants) inflate enough to explode? Two bras would be fitted separately to a cut-down mannequin for a simulated plane ride. As the air was sucked out of the chamber to replicate the pressure of 10,000 feet for the first bra test, the inflatable pockets expanded enough to knock the shoulder strap off the mannequin. But even at 40,000 feet (a dangerous altitude with extremely thin atmosphere), the bra lived on. After going beyond 70,000 feet, over twice the altitude at which a normal airliner would fly, no significant inflation or explosion occurred. While testing another bra—one with removable cups and less support—at 30,000 feet, there was still no explosion. Even at over 70,000 feet, nothing happened.

MYTH STATUS REVISITED: STILL BUSTED

The message remains reassuring for those with implants and inflatable undergarments. The flying public needn't fear any inflatable wardrobe malfunctions.

ADAM: "In altitudes above seventy thousand feet, you'd have other problems before you'd have to worry about any tightness on your breasts. If you're experiencing explosive decompression, your breasts are the least of your worries. You're going to die of hypoxia within ten seconds. Myth one hundred percent busted!"

Dealing from the bottom of the deck, the MythBusters pursue the case of . . .

The Killer Playing Card

THE PLAN: Playing cards can be thrown with a fair amount of force. Since the age of ten, Adam has been working to master the art of card throwing.

ADAM: "The first aspect is imparting lateral speed to the card. The second is imparting spin to it. It's the combination of both of those things that yields the most distance and stability."

Adam, as the mutant ninja card tosser, can make a jack of diamonds stick into a foam block target at the impressive speed of 25 miles per hour. Another expert celebrity card tosser is actor and sleight-of-hand specialist Ricky Jay. Ricky can flip a playing card nearly 200 feet, and his tosses can cut through newspaper or saw a cigarette right off your snout. But can somebody really be sliced and killed by a flying joker?

JAMIE: "We have unsubstantiated accounts that world-record-holding card throwers like Ricky Jay are throwing cards at almost ninety miles an hour. Our challenge in this myth was to build a machine that could throw a card as fast as possible."

THE EXPERIMENT: For starters, Jamie designed a nifty portable card-throwing device that was similar in principle to a mini baseball pitching machine. Jamie's handheld gadget turned out to be a card-throwing monster, pitching the ace of spades at a swift 70 mph.

The two main wheel-driven parts, which shot the card out of the machine, were made of hard rubber, and because of their 30,000 rpm topspin, Jamie soon

had to replace both wheel mechanisms with all-metal parts. As a result, the MythBusters' card-throwing gizmo was capable of launching the king of hearts at the blistering speed of 150 mph. At close range, Adam was capable of flinging a card roughly 0.25 inches into the foam target. But with Jamie's high-speed card chucker, half the surface of the playing card was embedded into the target.

But the question remained: Could Jamie's super card thrower deliver a deadly blow?

ADAM: "Creating a killer playing card isn't just about the speed. It also involves the mass. A single playing card weighs in at just one point seven grams."

For the final installment of the experiment, Adam and Jamie brought out a square block of ballistics gel in which to measure impact. Adam's best effort at card throwing penetrated the card into the gel only 0.25 inches. Jamie's 150-mph card chucker embedded his card only 0.5 inches. In contrast, a nonlethal pellet gun burrowed a slug 7 inches into the gel, and a heavy crossbow bolt shot at 200 mph penetrated the gel a deadly 20 inches.

 A card that penetrates ballistics gel only 0.5 inches is hardly the killing kind. In a last-ditch effort to draw blood, a shirtless Jamie (wearing eye protection) caught two rounds from the monster card chucker. He suffered two tiny cuts, one on his chest and the other on his arm.

So much for the myth of the killer playing card—that is, unless you can bleed to death from a mild paper cut. It seems the only killer card is the lucky one that wins a hand of five-card stud.

ADAM: "In spite of our über-machine, I didn't really see anything I thought was lethal from the playing cards. It just doesn't have enough mass, so I'm willing to say that this myth is pretty busted."

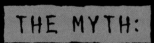

The MythBusters explore one of the Big Apple's most popular Empire State Building legends ever.

Penny Drop!

THE MYTH: They say that if a penny is thrown off a building the height of the Empire State Building, it will accelerate so fast that it will embed itself into the concrete at the base of the building—and if it were to hit somebody on the head, it'd kill them. This myth dates back to the late 1930s, when the Empire State Building first opened.

JAMIE: "The penny drop experiment shows how Adam and I work together. Sometimes we're working on the same thing, chipping in and getting a single task done. Other times we work separately. We like working separately—but in tandem—on one aspect of the project. Then we can consult and get feedback. In this case, I worked on the gun while Adam rigged a wind tunnel. We go back and forth, while eventually meeting together once all the components are done. We collaborate and rely on each other a great deal to make an experiment come to fruition."

THE PLAN: Tossing a coin off the Empire State Building is not as easy as it sounds. A tall building like that can generate its own unique weather conditions: Some updrafts can reach cyclonic speeds. Winds blowing against the face of the building can blow upward. It can even rain or snow up. Adam and Jamie, visiting the Empire State Building, noticed that by eight o'clock in the morning the wind was already capable of picking up objects on its own.

JAMIE: "There's every possibility that if you hurl a penny off the edge of a building the wind will just blow it back over."

120 mph

ADAM: "Still, how fast would a penny go if it fell one thousand two hundred and eighty feet, and what kind of damage would it do?"

Adam and Jamie needed to figure out what a penny's maximum speed is when falling, or in other words, its terminal velocity. Once they ascertained that, they would shoot pennies at concrete, asphalt, and a dummy head made from ballistics gel to see what kind of damage would be done.

The terminal velocity of a falling human is about 120 mph. But is a penny's the same? While parachuting out of an airplane, Adam let two handfuls of pennies fly. The coins flew upward in the wind currents, while Adam's body plummeted downward, proving that a 180-pound human has a higher terminal velocity than a penny weighing 2.5 grams.

Back at the workshop, Adam studied complex equations that put a penny's top speed at somewhere between 35 and 65 mph.

Then he built his own penny wind tunnel to test the coin's true terminal velocity. By running compressed air through a clear tube at the bottom of the wind tunnel, he was able to clock the wind speed at 65 mph. Holes in the upper part of the tube allowed the air to dissipate, so the wind speed dropped to 35 mph. A penny floated

freely inside Adam's mini wind-tunnel tube, proving that his equations were correct and making him one happy MythBuster. Without journeying back to the Empire State, he established a penny's correct terminal velocity, which the MythBusters decided to set at 65 mph.

ADAM: "One of my all-time favorite experiments. What's the terminal velocity of a penny? The penny has two different terminal velocities—one on its edge and one on the flat side. That makes it oscillate between thirty and sixty miles per hour. It would never fall faster than sixty-four miles per hour. So I built a wind tunnel that had a differential speed. At the base, it was sixty miles per hour; at its top it was thirty miles per hour. Once I tossed in a penny, the penny rode up and down the wind tunnel. You could see clearly how fast a penny would travel."

PETER: "Once we knew the top velocity, we needed to know if it could hurt someone. We needed a gun that could fire a penny at sixty-four miles per hour. Jamie came up with the simple solution of modifying a staple gun. We measured the speed. We tested to see if it could penetrate concrete or asphalt. We wanted to cover every aspect of the story."

Jamie figured out a way to fire a penny at high speed, using a normal woodshop staple gun and modifying the throat of the gun to shoot circular coins. After firing a few pennies, they tracked the propelled speed at 64.4 mph.

The MythBusters had figured out a surefire way to shoot a penny at the coin's highest terminal velocity of 65 mph.

The question remained, however: Could a 65-mph penny penetrate concrete, asphalt, or a human skull?

THE EXPERIMENT: It was time to see if Adam and Jamie's penny could achieve terminal velocity. The modified staple gun blasted the coin from 3 feet at a concrete block. The penny traveled the 3 feet in .032 seconds and left a small imprint. When the penny was launched at a block of asphalt, it bounced right off, proving that a coin traveling at terminal velocity cannot penetrate concrete or asphalt. But what about shattering someone's skull? When a penny was shot at the dummy cranium, although the coin broke through the thin layer of ballistics gel, the skull remained intact.

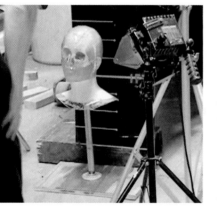

Jamie continued the experiment by aiming the high-velocity penny shooter at Adam's palm. It stung Adam's hand—twice—but no bruising or broken skin occurred.

ADAM: "Jamie took one of his staple guns and spent about fifteen minutes with a file modifying it, into which he popped a penny and shot me in the behind."

Though Adam was shot in the behind, there was no bruising—although nobody volunteered to check firsthand.

With the penny drop myth on shaky ground, the MythBusters took it one step further: What would happen if you shot a penny at the same velocity as a bullet? It was time to see how fast a penny had to go before it did some serious damage.

Adam modified a high-powered rifle so that it would expel a penny. The coin was fired from a specially designed aluminum barrel attached to the rifle like a silencer. The rifle itself was loaded with a blank round, and when it was fired, the expanding gases from the cartridge exploded along the barrel, propelling the coin from the slot at a bulletlike speed of 3,000 feet per second. It was a bold—and potentially deadly—plan, and it worked like a charm. The penny, shot from the slot at almost

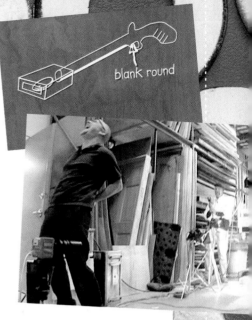

blank round

three times the speed of sound, left a definite imprint on the concrete. But the coin still didn't embed itself in the block. Even at supersonic speed, a penny weighing just 2.5 grams simply doesn't have enough mass to break through concrete or bone, unlike a real bullet, which is 6.65 millimeters of solid lead.

ADAM: "You need to test *all* the parameters in order to test the myth. What if you got a penny traveling as fast as humanly possible? What if there was no air and it fell off the Empire State Building? So we took that human cranium embedded inside ballistics gelatin and shot the penny at about twenty-five hundred miles per hour into the slime, and it still didn't pierce the bone. So we could definitively state that no matter how fast it's traveling, a penny does not have enough mass to actually kill you."

THE RESULT: Most coins thrown from the top of the Empire State Building don't get very far. They usually wind up just five stories down on an overhang at the eighty-first floor.

ADAM: "Still, if the penny *did* make it down to the street level, a two-and-a-half-gram penny doesn't have enough terminal velocity to kill a pedestrian below."

JAMIE: "The worst thing I could come up with is if you were looking straight up in the sky and got hit in the eye. Even then, I don't know whether it would take your eye out. Sixty-four miles an hour wasn't enough to cause any kind of damage to a person. Then when we made it go almost three times the speed of sound, it still wasn't enough to break bones."

ADAM: "The penny drop myth isn't worth a dime. I think we busted the heck out of this one. Myth busted."

SCIENTIFIC PRINCIPLE

PETER: "The scientific principles covered in this experiment included terminal velocity and wind resistance. There's a NASA group who have a simulated zero-g facility where they can drop things down a five-hundred-foot tower, but the thing that Adam and I were most enthusiastic about was that Adam came up with this incredibly simple, elegant model that explained terminal velocity."

ADAM: "And of course, the coup de grace was that you couldn't drop a penny off the Empire State Building. Unless you can throw a penny the length of a football field—that's the distance from the observation deck to the street, horizontally—it will never reach the street. Five stories below the observation deck, off the eighty-first floor, there's tons of coins all around the perimeter from people throwing change."

Is Hollywood telling us the truth? Will a car really explode if you shoot its gas tank? There are more than 600 million cars in the world today, and many myths about them. Sounds like fertile ground for a pair of MythBusting motormouths.

MythBusters Car Capers

THE MYTHS: There are all sorts of myths having to do with automobiles, so the MythBusters secured themselves an old donated car they dubbed Earl.

PETER: "Car Capers was an example of a series of myths that even we believed. It's a great surprise when we bust a myth that we believe in. That's why it's funny to test a myth that everybody believes, but nobody bothers to test."

MOTORING MYTH #1: Tailpipe Terrors

It's a classic college prank to block a car's tailpipe with a piece of food. But will that really cause the car to stall? With the car's big engine, Jamie surmised, whatever the MythBusters put up the exhaust pipe would probably come out pretty quickly. With a high-speed camera trained on Earl's tailpipe, a wide collection of food props was fired from the car.

Adam selected the ammo. The first, a potato, was stuffed 20 inches into the tailpipe, resulting in a potato projectile with no effect on the engine. A banana, longer and thinner, did no better: It slipped right out. How about an egg? The egg was shot airborne, but it didn't stall the car. Whatever foodstuff the MythBusters stuffed up the tailpipe came right back out again.

FINAL VERDICT: TOTALLY BUSTED

MOTORING MYTH #2: Unauthorized Additives

Engine additives are designed to improve a car's performance. But MythBusters additives are a little different. In order to test these "additive" myths, Jamie and Adam pulled the engine out of the car and added a see-through gas tank that, because of the fire risk, remained separate from the engine. Blast screens were erected around the engine for safety purposes as well.

First Additive Myth: CAN DRAIN CLOG REMOVER POURED INTO THE GAS TANK MAKE THE ENGINE EXPLODE?

After the clog remover went in and time passed, the car's engine was still purring. The idle speed hadn't changed at all. Nothing happened.

ADAM: "A distinct lack of explosion."

Second Additive Myth:
WHAT HAPPENS WHEN YOU ADD BLEACH TO AN ENGINE?

After pouring household bleach into the gas tank, Jamie revved the motor. Everything ran fine until the engine cut out. After circulating through the engine, the bleach stopped the car from running. By the next morning, the bleach—an oxidizing agent—had rusted the inside of the gas tank.

FINAL VERDIC PLAUSIBLE

Third Additive Myth: WILL ADDING SUGAR TO THE GAS TANK CAUSE A CAR TO BLOW UP?

Didn't happen. Even left overnight, the engine started immediately the next day.

FINAL VERDIC TOTALLY BUSTED

Fourth Additive Myth: DOES PUTTING MOTHBALLS IN YOUR GASOLINE CREATE A HIGH-OCTANE FUEL IN YOUR ENGINE?

After Adam poured a gasoline and mothball mixture into the tank, there *was* a gradual change in the engine's performance. At first it sputtered, but then there was a notable transformation. The engine actually sounded more powerful. The MythBusters showed that a few mothballs in the tank seemed to increase the octane of gas. However, they don't recommend using mothballs as an additive, since they may have a negative effect on other parts of the engine.

FINAL VERDIC PLAUSIBLE

PETER: "What we should have done was let some of these experiments sit. Sugar in the gas tank doesn't stop the engine from running, but it might if you left it in there for forty-eight hours."

JAMIE: "That was the nature of the feedback I got as well. We needed to let some of that stuff set for a while."

MOTORING MYTH #3: Shooting Cars

First Car Shooting Myth:
WILL SHOOTING A CAR'S GAS TANK BLOW UP THE CAR?

The MythBusters car helped Jamie and Adam put a very famous Hollywood myth to rest. In countless action movies, a well-placed slug causes a spectacular detonation of an auto. Using a scope rifle to test the myth, Jamie expertly shot the car's full gas tank with a tight cluster of five bullet holes. But there was no explosion, even after all five shots passed right through to the other side of the tank.

FINAL VERDICT BUSTED

Second Car Shooting Myth: WILL HIDING BEHIND A CAR DOOR PROTECT YOU FROM BULLETS IN A GUN BATTLE?

Another popular Hollywood myth is that hiding behind a car door will stop you from getting shot. The myth was thoroughly tested when fifty rounds were fired into the driver's door. Like the ending of *Bonnie and Clyde*, the car was littered with bullets. The gunfire went straight through the car door's paneling, tearing up the car's interior.

ADAM: "I think we can safely say that unlike in the movies, being behind a car door during a gunfight is *not* a safe place to be. The best advice is not to get into a gunfight!"

FINAL VERDICT: **BUSTED**

MOTORING MYTH #4: Roadside Rescues

First Roadside Rescue Myth: IF YOU HAVE A BONE-DRY RADIATOR, CAN YOU START THE CAR SAFELY BY PUTTING COLA IN YOUR COOLING SYSTEM?

After draining the radiator, Adam refilled it with his favorite soft drink, MythBusters Cola. After the car started, it seemed to be enjoying its cola refreshment. Earl ran normally; however, after the engine was turned off, the car experienced a little minor backpressure from the carbonation.

FINAL VERDICT: PLAUSIBLE

SAFETY NOTE

☠ The MythBusters know that all firearms are dangerous and should only be used responsibly and in a safe environment. Do not try this at home!

Second Roadside Rescue Myth:

WILL CRACKING AN EGG INTO A LEAKY RADIATOR HELP PLUG UP A HOLE?

After puncturing the radiator with an ice pick and creating a steady leak, an egg was cracked into the radiator. Voilà! The radiator continued to leak for a short time until something egg-straordinary occurred: The leak stopped, showing that an egg just might work better than the commercial remedy.

FINAL VERDIC   MAYBE NOT A PERMANENT SOLUTION, BUT CERTAINLY PLAUSIBLE

MOTORING MYTH #5: Engine Terminators

First Engine Terminator Myth:

IF A PIECE OF METAL AS TINY AS A PENNY IS DROPPED INTO AN ENGINE'S CARBURETOR, WILL IT DESTROY THE ENGINE?

With a penny inside the carburetor, the engine was revved repeatedly. While the penny knocked around noisily inside the engine, it didn't ruin the engine.

FINAL VERDIC   BUSTED

Second Engine Terminator Myth:

CAN ADDING BLEACH INTO THE ENGINE OIL RUIN THE LUBRICATION, CAUSING THE ENGINE TO HEAT UP, SEIZE UP, AND EVENTUALLY DIE?

Putting bleach in the gas tank was supposed to stop the engine, and it did. But putting bleach in the oil was meant to destroy the engine. After MythBusters Bleach was poured into the engine oil, the engine smoked, overheated, and sang its death song. The fumes, noise, and smell generated were horrible, and the engine finally died.

FINAL VERDIC   PLAUSIBLE

If you're flying in an airplane, which kind of fowl coming at you is more destructive, frozen or thawed?

Chicken Gun:
Frozen or Thawed?

THE MYTH: It's no secret that scientists conduct impact tests by firing bird carcasses from big guns—virtual chicken cannons, which test how an airplane's windshield will hold up against a splattered bird hit. With more than 3,000 bird strikes each year, aviation authorities spend millions trying to protect cockpit crews.

JAMIE: "The original myth stated that the British borrowed chicken gun technology from NASA in order to test the impact of bird hits on high-speed trains. But they ran into a problem when the chickens were going right through the windshields of the trains, even embedding themselves in the seats farther down inside the train. Of course the British were horrified, so they sent a tape back to NASA asking for help. NASA simply replied, 'Gentlemen, thaw your chickens.'"

161

The MythBusters' mission was to determine not whether there was a chicken gun in existence, but whether or not there's a difference in the impact of a frozen or thawed chicken traveling at high velocity through an airplane windshield.

PETER: "The way we should have originally framed the experiment was, 'Is there a point at which one will penetrate and the other won't?' which is the essence of the myth."

THE PLAN: To fire thawed or frozen chickens at high speed, the MythBusters needed a sealed tank and a compressor to supply compressed air for their massive homemade chicken gun. An industrial-strength butterfly valve provided the explosive release for firing the chicken carcasses down a long metal pipe barrel. The target? A used plane fuselage cut from a small aircraft with several spare windshields.

After obtaining a piece of light aircraft fuselage, Adam found the ideal tank, which could be filled with the proper amount of compressed air. Then Jamie found an oversized butterfly valve, which would release the pressurized air through several feet of 10-inch-diameter, 0.25-inch steel pipe, which acted as a barrel.

JAMIE: "After we cut the pipe to length and cut a hole in the tank for the barrel to fit into for the explosive release of air, the butterfly valve was fitted between two additional lengths of pipe. The large butterfly valve was the most critical aspect of the chicken gun, the only mechanism standing between a great shot and a weak one. Yet once the tank was filled with pressurized air at two hundred psi, and after the butterfly valve was opened, chickens were soon flying out of the barrel."

The MythBusters' Chicken Gun was ready to test the validity of the myth.

Adam and Jamie's ammunition was four frozen and four thawed chickens. In order to launch the too-small chickens explosively, they had to fit inside the barrel snugly. Using expanding rigid foam, Adam constructed a sleeve called a sabot, a perfectly molded cartridge into which the chickens could be snugly slipped and thus be the size of the barrel.

ADAM: "The chicken gun now had all the basic ingredients—a tank, a valve, and a barrel—excellently welded together. The plane fuselage was set inside a blast chamber. The chickens were ready to be properly and powerfully propelled toward the aircraft windshields."

THE EXPERIMENT: With the tank's air pressure primed, Adam and Jamie shot frozen and thawed chicken carcasses to compare any marked difference in their impact on the windshields. As the chickens flew, they were clocked at 121 mph. Both frozen and thawed made equal mincemeat of the scrap windshields and seemed to travel at very similar speeds. Then the MythBusters tried reducing the tank pressure to 50 psi. Would there be a difference upon impact between frozen and thawed at a slower speed? What would the slower speed be? Blasting another frozen bird with less pressure, it flew at 128 mph. At the same pressure, 50 psi, a thawed bird was clocked at 132 mph. Cutting the pressure to 25 psi, the MythBusters still found their flying poultry, frozen or thawed, to be equally destructive, traveling at virtually the same speed. Changing the internal pressure of the tank didn't seem to slow down the chickens at all.

JAMIE: "Then came a hitch—and a potentially fatal flaw—in our Chicken Gun experiment. While testing which chicken hits hardest, frozen or thawed, the MythBusters discovered, to their horror, that their light aircraft windshields weren't officially rated for bird strikes. Nothing had been proven."

In order to lay this myth to rest, Adam and Jamie rethought their methodology. No more windshields. They would purely measure each chicken's moment of impact.

ADAM: "Chickens were fired at a solid steel plate, and by using a high-speed camera to measure the time between the start and finish of impact, we held out hope that we might see a difference between frozen and thawed chickens. After the three frozen chickens were clocked at over one hundred forty miles per hour, impact was measured at .0007 of a second. Impact times for the three thawed chickens showed a perfect match, .0007 of a second as well."

The results, substantiated by the high-speed photography, were fairly convincing. Hitting the plate was when the force was imparted. Both the frozen and the thawed chickens had the same mass and effectively the same speed. The only difference between the two chickens might be how much time it took for them to impart their energy to the metal plate. But with the high-speed camera, the MythBusters showed that each of them exerted all their energy in 7 milliseconds.

MYTH STATUS:
BUSTED?

There was no difference in impact between the frozen and thawed chickens at the speeds measured. Myth busted.

BUT WAIT! CHICKEN GUN, FROZEN OR THAWED? RESULTS REVISITED:

PETER: "The initial busting of the Chicken Gun myth didn't sit well with some viewers. The data seemed flawed. First, after finding out that the windshields weren't rated for bird strikes, Adam and Jamie tried shooting thawed and frozen chickens at a steel plate, timing the impact. More viewers complained. What counted wasn't the timing, but the penetration. Jamie, especially, remained skeptical. He firmly believed that a frozen chicken had to have more penetration than a thawed one. So it was back to the MythBusters drawing board."

After a futile and inconclusive attempt at firing more thawed and frozen chickens into blocks of foam, Adam was convinced there was still no difference. But to Jamie, the MythBusters' data remained inconclusive and random. After a third experiment involving more blocks of foam, the MythBusters were temporarily stymied. Jamie was still confident that frozen packed more punch. Adam was not so sure.

ADAM: "This was a key education for us. Once we tried the wrong airplane windshield, and then the metal plate outdoors, we came to understand that what we really needed was a result where one was positive and one negative and why there was a difference between the two, and if it conformed to Jamie's expectations. It took four tries to get something that finally made sense."

JAMIE: "For the fourth experiment, chickens were shot at a wooden box containing twelve sheets of quarter-inch glass. The more panes broken, we figured, the more penetration power. Firing remotely, the first thawed chicken shattered two panes. The frozen chicken, however, dramatically blasted a hole through all twelve panes of glass. My obstinacy paid off as the findings were finally revised."

MYTH STATUS REVISITED: PLAUSIBLE

JAMIE: "After four separate attempts, we've finally overturned our original analysis of the Chicken Gun Myth. We can clearly say this one is now totally plausible. Frozen chickens outpenetrate thawed ones."

The MythBusters drink up for science.

You Can't Beat the Breath Test!

THE MYTH: Is it possible to beat a Breathalyzer test when legally intoxicated? Lots of strange myths have surfaced about all the substances that can potentially beat the breath test.

THE PLAN: Jamie and Adam reported to the San Francisco Police Department Crime Lab to test up against a Breathalyzer machine. A police officer watched over Adam and Jamie as they got themselves too drunk to legally operate a motor vehicle.

ADAM: "We also filmed an episode about the hazards of drunken driving versus using a cell phone while driving. For that experiment, they made sure to have us not eat the entire day so we would have empty stomachs. It

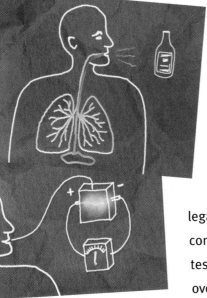

was very efficient. Within an hour, four beers got me to just under the legal limit and we were able to do the experiment. For the Breathalyzer experiment, we had eaten breakfast and we ate lunch in the middle. Jamie and I polished off thirteen drinks. We were both pulling about a 'one' by the time they tested us."

In California someone is considered legally intoxicated with a blood alcohol concentration of .08. Adam blew into the breath-tester and his blood alcohol level read at .11, well over the limit. Jamie, because of the difference in his muscle mass, processed his alcohol more efficiently. He tested at .09, still too drunk to be legally behind the wheel.

To prove a driver is drunk, police usually rely on a breath test. The Breathalyzer was invented in the 1950s. Breath tests work because alcohol is carried by the blood into the lungs and exhaled. The amount of alcohol on a person's breath is proportional to the amount in the bloodstream. Some machines rely on chemical reaction. Some act like a fuel cell, wherein the more alcohol that's blown in, the higher the electrical current that's produced. A third kind uses infrared light to find alcohol molecules.

JAMIE: "Spirits are about forty percent alcohol. How many drinks needed to reach the legal limit of drunkenness depends largely on a person's weight and how fast one drinks. Food slows alcohol's absorption into the bloodstream,  while just five percent of alcohol is expelled through urine. Since the liver can only metabolize one drink per hour, the body can't keep up with the consumption of large amounts of alcohol."

THE EXPERIMENT:

While legally intoxicated, Adam and Jamie used a few products which, according to urban myths, are said to be capable of confusing the breath-testing machine.

* Consuming breath mints: Adam tests at .10.

* Biting into a raw onion: Jamie scores a .08.

* A battery in the mouth to offset the electrical reading: Adam scores a .10.

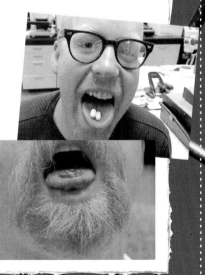

* Copper pennies in the mouth to throw off the chemical balance: Jamie scores a .09.

* Swilling mouthwash or using denture cream: Adam scores a .11.

THE RESULT: After numerous drinks and a mouthful of onion, batteries, pennies, mouthwash, and denture cream, Adam and Jamie proved a sobering warning for any potential drunk driver. You can't beat the breath test!

MYTH STATUS: BUSTED

ADAM: "This myth is definitively busted. You can't beat the breath test! Even if they got two readings that were grossly out of synch, a blood test would tell them exactly how much alcohol you have in your system. It would seem that nothing works."

PETER: "This video is currently being used by the California Highway Patrol and police academies all over. What was funny during this experiment was that Adam told bad cop jokes during the tests, with the San Francisco Police Department standing there!"

SAFETY NOTE

☠ Don't drink and drive. Forty percent of American road deaths involve alcohol, and 17,000 people are killed each year at the hands of drunk drivers.

The Great Cement Truck Mix-Up

The MythBusters are hot on the trail of one dynamite construction industry myth.

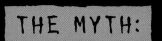

THE MYTH: Can you remove the buildup of concret e from a cement truck by blasting the inner barrel with dynamite?

There are a number of different versions of this myth. Some involve clearing the inside of a cement truck barrel with cherry bombs, dynamite, or more.

ADAM: "I could see this actually working as long as you didn't put too much dynamite in there, [otherwise] the whole truck is gone. But if you did it just right, the shock wave would probably release the concrete from the surface of the metal drum."

The MythBusters team began by visiting a cement-mixing site and obtaining an old cement truck that had gone way past its sell-by date. According to those in the concrete industry, the normal way to clean the inside barrel of a cement truck is to send two laborers inside with chisels and chippers. The process takes a whole day to complete. Incidentally, in the concrete delivery trade, a truck driver has ninety minutes to drop off the load; otherwise, the entire mixture inside will harden. The cardinal sin of any cement truck driver would be to get stuck in traffic and allow that to happen.

PETER: "Our researcher got us the cement trucks for free. He's also gotten us two boom lifts and the sixty thousand free Ping-Pong balls. It's funny what people will offer a television show. Jamie was once sitting on a plane next to one of the managing directors of a company that manufactures fighting vehicles. He offered us the use of one, which we eventually used to drag a four-thousand-pound shark."

Two cement trucks were used in the experiment. The first, christened Twister #1, was inadvertently overfilled and ended up with half a load of hardened concrete. The second truck, Twister #2, contained the precise amount of light coating inside the barrel to conduct the original experiment.

ADAM: "We have two myths to bust here. One is the myth of the guy trying to dislodge an ungodly slab. And the other is somebody just trying to clean it out. This sufficed for both."

THE EXPERIMENT:

The experiment evolved into a twofold operation. The original plan was to load Twister #2 with a small amount of concrete—just enough concrete to coat the barrel with 3 or 4 inches, let it harden, then blow up the inner barrel. Adam and Jamie then had a pyrotechnician suspend and detonate a stick and a half of dynamite inside the lightly coated barrel.

Did they blow the cement off without destroying the truck?

During the blast, high-speed cameras showed the moment of concussion when expanding air shook loose a lot of the concrete slag.

JAMIE: "Upon closer inspection, many big chunks were loosened from the barrel without doing major damage to the rest of the vehicle. A huge amount of crumbled concrete was extracted, and what was left on the inside walls was pretty loose."

THE RESULT: The MythBusters proceeded with Twister #1, filling it with 6 cubic yards of dried concrete, which formed a 4-foot concrete slab floor inside the barrel. Cherry bombs failed to shake it loose. So did a 1-pound black powder bomb (a blast equivalent to a half stick of dynamite). It was quickly determined that no amount of explosives could blow the concrete loose without obliterating the entire vehicle.

So why not just blow up the whole darned truck?

And that's exactly what the MythBusters did. Twister #1 would mark the largest detonation blast in the team's short history.

Adam and Jamie brought a virtual wrecking crew to a rural site in Calaveras County, California. It was time to blow Twister #1 to kingdom come—with their frontline team and a truckload of high explosives, plus paramedics, firefighters, and bomb technicians standing by.

With the help of a retired FBI explosives specialist, 850 pounds of a commercial blasting agent (the same mixture used for quarrying) were loaded inside the truck's barrel through an access panel cut into its side. Dozens of bags of high explosives were charged and ready for the big boom. An exclusion zone was put up around the blast site. All roads were sealed off within a 1-mile radius of the blast. Only one digital camera operator, stationed behind a blast screen, was allowed within the zone.

Fire in the hole!

After a 10-second countdown, a massive blast erupted (causing Jamie to jump), followed by a strong aftershock. The cement truck completely evaporated from sight.

ADAM: "This is crazy. It's all gone. No more truck. MythBusters 1, cement truck 0."

JAMIE: "I had never seen a blast that big before. It was really impressive. Talk about removing concrete. There is no concrete. There is no truck. No nothing."

MYTH STATUS: PLAUSIBLE

The MythBusters proved the original myth "plausible" when they managed to clean concrete slag from the barrel of Twister #2 with dynamite.

ADAM: "That myth is *totally* plausible and to tell you the truth, if I were a cement truck driver and I had to clean out my truck, I would probably try this first. Jackhammering in there does not sound like a lot of fun."

As for Twister #1 being blasted off the face of the earth with 850 pounds of high explosives, that experiment went way beyond the realm of urban mythology.

JAMIE: "That's what we do on *MythBusters*. We take large objects and make them into very small objects."

SAFETY NOTE

☠ Never play with illegal fireworks. As usual, don't try any of this at home. These guys are trained experts with a safety team behind them.

JAMIE: "In terms of the MythBusters using high explosives, we learned from hard experience that we need to respect the instructions from the experts in explosives."

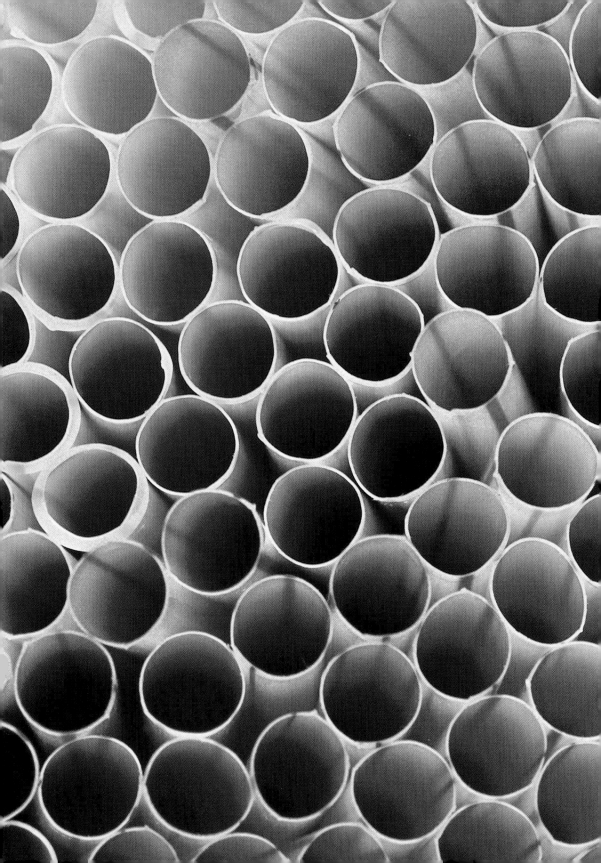

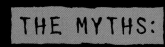

Put the cola down....

MythBusters
Cola Myths

THE MYTHS: There are plenty of legends associated with cola. Some of them sound feasible while others seem absolutely ridiculous. In lieu of explosions and grand-scale MythBuster experiments, a simple lab test debunking or supporting the properties of carbonated cola seemed in order.

COLA MYTH #1: Can Cola Clean Up Blood?

Can cola shift those hard-to-remove bloodstains from a MythBusters crime scene? Animal blood, used to keep the test as authentic as possible, was spilled out onto the pavement. After two hours in the California sun, Jamie and Adam cleaned the pavement and a truck bumper with cola.

FINAL VERDICT: The cola worked well on the bumper, but didn't do much on the pavement.

COLA MYTH #2: Can Cola Polish Chrome?

Here's another unusual household myth: Will cola applied with aluminum foil shine up the chrome on your car? The MythBusters compared cola against a leading brand of chrome cleaner. According to Jamie's tests, the cola did a better job. The rust on the truck bumper was all gone after the foaming bubble effects of the cola lifted the rust off the chrome. It left a sticky mess, but one that easily washed off.

FINAL VERDICT: Both Jamie and Adam agree unanimously: Cola is a fantastic chrome cleaner.

COLA MYTH #3: Does Cola Loosen Stuck Rusty Bolts?

The myth claims that a cola-soaked rag will help loosen a rusty bolt. Will cola's low phosphoric acid content be effective against the rust buildup? After five minutes, the cola seemed to have little or no effect.

FINAL VERDICT: A total failure with very little penetration. The cola may have removed a little surface rust, but the bolt was not loosened.

Phosphoric acid, an active ingredient in cola, gives the drink its sharp taste. Most food contains natural acid, much of it stronger than phosphoric, so how will the cola react versus phosphoric acid on the following chosen test items?

COLA MYTH #4: Can Cola Shine a Penny?

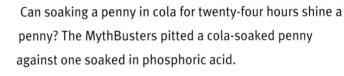

Can soaking a penny in cola for twenty-four hours shine a penny? The MythBusters pitted a cola-soaked penny against one soaked in phosphoric acid.

FINAL VERDICT: The cola cleans pennies more effectively than the acid. The myth is true.

COLA MYTH #5: Can Cola Erode a Tooth?

Will a tooth left soaking overnight in cola dissolve? While the cola did make the tooth turn "a yucky brown," the phosphoric acid was measurably more effective in dissolving the tooth, eating half of the whitened tooth away.

FINAL VERDICT: In a twenty-four-hour period, cola could never dissolve a tooth. Myth busted.

COLA MYTH #6: Can Cola Dissolve a Steak?

The MythBusters "marinated" two raw T-bone steaks—one in cola and one in phosphoric acid—for forty-eight hours. Which would dissolve the steak? After more than two days, the phosphoric acid significantly broke down the steak, while the cola left the steak intact in a fine glaze of mold, nothing even remotely dissolved off the bone. (Jamie observed, however, that the cola might have tenderized the steak a little.)

FINAL VERDICT: Cola does little or nothing to a steak. Myth busted.

COLA MYTH #8: Can Cola Clean Battery Terminals?

Using an old battery as a test, the MythBusters tried cleaning the corroded terminals with cola and a brush, baking soda and a toothbrush, and plain water and a rag.

FINAL VERDICT: No major difference. The cola worked by virtue of its being a liquid, but did not have any special anticorrosive properties.

COLA MYTH #10: Can Cola Double as a Grease Stain Remover?

After greasing up Jamie's coveralls with engine grease and oil, cut cloth samples were then soaked separately in cola and a leading brand of detergent for four days.

FINAL VERDICT: After rinsing, neither unagitated bits of cloth were cleansed of the grease, and the cola had turned the white material brown.

COLA MYTH #9: Can Cola Degrease an Engine?

The MythBusters attempted to clean a greasy automobile engine by dousing it with straight cola and letting it sit for ten minutes.

FINAL VERDICT: While the cola cleaned off a lot of the dirt, the grease remained intact. Cola may have removed a little bit of corrosion, but not much. Cola as an engine degreaser is a busted myth.

COLA MYTH #7: Can Cola Ruin a Car Paint Job?

In this test, cola competed against concentrated phosphoric acid. Both were poured down the side of Jamie's truck and left to sit for twenty-four hours.

FINAL VERDICT:
The phosphoric acid bleached the white paint job and ate through the paint. The cola wasn't nearly as effective in ruining the paint job. Another cola myth busted.

Adam and Jamie face the music! The MythBusters search high and low for the elusive bowel-loosening tone.

In Search of the Brown Note

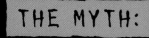

THE MYTH: This myth states that there are subsonic sound frequencies that you can play or reproduce that will cause human beings to lose control of their bowels or experience what's called "involuntary bowel motility."

The Brown Note is a mysterious sound that is supposed to make you soil your pants—or worse! Conspiracy theories dating back to World War II claim that shady government types have secretly researched this phenomenon for all sorts of no good.

ADAM: "According to the myth, if you can get the right subsonic frequencies and vibrations hitting your body the right way, it brings on nausea, cold sweat, confusion, a head full of pressure, and a loss of bowel control."

THE PLAN: The MythBusters headed into a world of hertz with twenty-four speakers and $60,000 worth of sound equipment. Putting their dignity on the line, a crew of fourteen adults, including sound specialists, donned diapers in an attempt to uncover the most diabolical secret weapon in the world of audio—the dreaded Brown Note!

Sounds are merely vibrations, while the speed of those vibrations is known as the frequency. Frequencies are measured in hertz (Hz). One vibration per second equals 1 Hz. There have been reports of the Brown Note appearing within the 5-, 7-, 8-, and 9-Hz range, all frequencies below the range of human hearing. People can't hear sounds much lower than 20 Hz, while the Brown Note allegedly falls below the 10 Hz range.

The MythBusters' plan was simple. Arrange specially modified speakers around a subject, then hit him (or her) with tones until the Brown Note reared its ugly head. The twenty-four speakers, driven by 25,000 watts of power, formed the ultimate surround sound system that could easily double as a complete subwoofer system for a large touring rock show.

With tons of audio technology aimed straight at him, Adam volunteered to potentially go potty on national TV. While Adam faced the music, a medical team constantly monitored his physical signs. (Don't try this at home!) They were prepared for the worst: A possible change of pressure or some other kind of neurological response that would make Adam lose control of his bowels. And since the Brown Note was said to also induce confusion, Adam—while standing in front of the barrage of loud sound waves—performed a timed puzzle designed to measure any disorientation or confusion.

JAMIE: "As a final precaution, Adam—and everyone else standing nearby the omnidirectional Brown Note signal—wore diapers, Superman-style, on the outside of their pants. After donning his diaper, Adam faced the mysterious repercussions of the Brown Note."

THE EXPERIMENT:

The Meyer Sound experts first blasted Adam with a 5-Hz tone, well below the frequency of the human ear. It packed quite a subsonic punch, thumping out a whopping 108 decibels (dB). (A rock concert is usually about 110 dBs, while a normal conversation is rated at about 60 dBs.) Adam remained unmoved, while his heart rate remained the same. There was no sign of confusion, either. Adam's bowels were more than a match for the 5-Hz blast.

Next came 7 Hz at 114 dB. Although the silence was deafening, there was still no involuntary reaction from Adam's nether regions.

Then they tried 9 Hz at 114 dB, right within range of the mystical Brown Note frequency. Still no pay dirt. However, there was a little collateral damage: Those standing within range of the speakers began to feel physical symptoms in their chests in the form of anxiety, upset stomach, nausea, dizziness, and light-headedness.

Finally, Adam, donning ear protection, was blasted with 32 Hz at 128 dB, way up into the audible range of humans, emulating a sound as loud as a jackhammer. Adam could feel pressure on his chest and his eyeballs, but still no involuntary pile of poo.

As a last-ditch attempt to smoke out the Brown Note, a final dose of power was added. The Meyer Sound guys aggressively swept a series of long wavelengths and frequencies up and down between 20 and 100 Hz at 154 dB.

ADAM: "The sound patterns physically moved air in and out of my lungs as I breathed. The frequency sweeps were louder than a jet aircraft taking off and were powerful enough to rupture unprotected eardrums. The feeling was a lot like someone drumming on my chest. It was absolutely amazing, but still no Brown Note."

THE RESULT:

Despite the incredibly powerful audio barrage on Adam, there was not a single sign of any lost bowel control. Adam's dignity remained intact.

MYTH STATUS:

JAMIE: "It seems the military can save itself some trouble. Even with the help of some of the world's best audio technicians blasting sound frequencies in the five-, seven-, and nine-Hz range, we could not reproduce the Brown Note. The Brown Note Myth was busted!"

Faster drives, shattering results, and danger at your home computer. Are CDs spinning toward destruction?

Exploding CDs?

THE MYTH: The myth is that new, extremely high-speed CD drives may actually exceed the structural capabilities of the CDs they drive, causing the discs to explode and shatter into many pieces . . . sometimes even leaving the computer and endangering the user.

In order to test the myth, the MythBusters sped up several CDs under different conditions and got them to explode in all sorts of spectacular ways. In addition to driving discs inside a computer drive, the MythBusters adapted some high-speed tools to spin the CDs beyond 30,000 rpm and cause them to experience critical failure. The process was dangerous—sharp fragments of polycarbonate can travel at speeds in excess of 700 mph. So the MythBusters used a special ballistics dummy to sit behind a blast chamber in front of the computer drive in order to test whether or not such fragments can penetrate human skin.

JAMIE: "CD manufacturers are aware of the myth of the exploding CDs. Much of it relates to a single article written by a PC journalist in Sweden, who tested CDs at thirty thousand rpm, which approximated the force and speed of a 52x CD-ROM drive. Despite the article, such an occurrence has been difficult to duplicate."

ADAM: "This situation happens constantly on the show. We're dealing with something that's a once-in-a-long-shot thing. Just as I seriously doubt we'll ever get a cell phone battery to explode on the show, when maybe eight have exploded out of the zillions that have been sold. But with the CD-ROM thing, a week doesn't go by that someone doesn't e-mail me that a CD has broken inside his or her computer. I guess every time it happens to someone in the world, I get an e-mail."

JAMIE: "In order to replicate the CD-shattering experience, Adam exposed some average computer discs to the kind of treatment normally imposed on them by users. CDs that allegedly blew apart inside computer drives may have been damaged by sunlight, corrosive spills, or normal wear and tear. In order to test this myth realistically, a few CDs were cracked, exposed to sunlight for twenty-four hours, doused with rubbing alcohol, fried in the microwave, and their labels were stuck on off-center. Also, an undamaged, expensive name brand served as the control CD."

23,000 rpm

Speed was the key in busting this myth. Computer drives rated at 52x usually spin CDs at around 30,000 rpm. While some discs disintegrated at this point, others required much higher stresses in order to induce failure. What was needed was more speed.

Jamie's quest for speed involved adapting electrical hand tools and fitting

CDs into places they weren't meant to go. Meanwhile, Adam created a ballistics dummy that was placed in the shatter zone for a dramatic demonstration of possible injury. The dummy was made from gelatin, a substance which, when set, closely matches human skin and flesh.

THE EXPERIMENT: What did it take to shatter a CD on a drive? Since the ordinary computer towers in which MythBusters originally tested their discs could achieve less than 20,000 rpm, Jamie hatched another plan. He built the equivalent of a 300x speed drive. Jamie's customized drive added more power to the equation by adapting a superfast motor plugged into a variable speed controller. The motor was set up to revolve as fast as 90,000 rpm. Fortunately, it was safely contained within a blast chamber in case Jamie's drive became as dangerous as an exploding CD. Revving CDs up to demolition speed became the aim.

PETER: "We knew this story was true. The question was, how were we going to reproduce it? Such a tiny percentage of CDs actually break, we could have spun off a hundred thousand CDs and maybe one might have gone. The first attempt was in a CD-ROM drive. We just couldn't get the bloody thing to go thirty thousand rpm, which is where the CDs were supposed to be breaking.

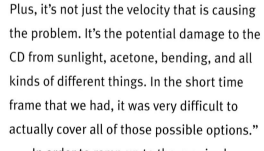

Plus, it's not just the velocity that is causing the problem. It's the potential damage to the CD from sunlight, acetone, bending, and all kinds of different things. In the short time frame that we had, it was very difficult to actually cover all of those possible options."

In order to ramp up to the required 30,000 rpm, the MythBusters turned to the shop's other fast tools. Lathe: 2,000 rpm. Bench grinder: 3,500 rpm. Drill: 60,000 rpm. However, since none of those tools proved suitable as a simulated drive, the team purchased a tougher, faster router in order to direct-drive the test CDs. Adam's initial fear was that the CD fried inside the microwave would not withstand the forces, and he was right. What happened to the ballistics dummy? A horror show! Several stray pieces of shattered CD were found embedded as deeply as 2 inches into the dummy's flesh.

Then Jamie and Adam achieved more mass destruction. By switching from 110 volts to a more potent 220 volts, they created a monster drive. Loading the CDs was a shattering ordeal, creating shards of flying disc shrapnel from behind the safety of the MythBusters' blast shield. (Don't try this at home.)

So what does the future hold? Will faster disc drives create danger in front of home computers?

THE RESULT: Even if a CD blew up inside your computer, could you be at risk?

ADAM: "The answer is no; that is, unless you opened up your hard drive and got ridiculously close to the disc. In other words, computer users needn't worry about exploding CDs and flying fragments. During the MythBusters' experiment, most undamaged control CDs withstood standard spin forces. Only one disc disintegrated, warping but not shattering."

JAMIE: "In the future, even if high-speed 52x and 56x drives cause some discs to shatter, according to storage experts, what we'll probably see in terms of increased capacity is the use of different types of lasers and technology. Thus, disc speed will not be a critical issue and drives probably won't have to exceed 52x in order to accomplish their functions."

MYTH STATUS: BUSTED

ADAM: "Given the millions and millions of CDs out there being burned, and considering the dozen cases of them reportedly shattering, this myth sounds like a nonevent, not something the average computer user needs to worry about. Highly unlikely."

Forty-two *Luftballons*: Could it really happen? Did a man tether forty-two weather balloons to his lawn chair and fly sixteen thousand feet?

Larry's Lawn Chair Balloon

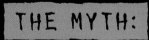

THE MYTH: A story that made it onto the Internet a few years ago featured a man named Larry Walters, who supposedly flew above LAX in 1982 after attaching over forty weather balloons to a lawn chair. For snacks on his unconventional flight, he took along sandwiches and beef jerky. According to the myth, Larry—an unemployed truck driver at the time—shot up over 16,000 feet straight into the air and flew for fourteen hours. Larry's plan was to descend and land by shooting out some of the weather balloons with a BB gun. Then a helicopter allegedly rescued him.

ADAM: "This was the very first myth we ever shot. I remember that because we'd been doing prep for two and a half weeks, and we decided to start two days earlier because I flew exactly on the twentieth anniversary of Larry Walters's original flight."

PETER: "We knew it was true. Some people criticized us for doing a true story. Yet while a lot of people on the West Coast of the U.S. know that it's a true story, throughout the rest of the world it's taken on mythic status. We replicated exactly what Larry did, except I think that Larry used brand-new weather balloons, and for some reason we got ex-military balloons that were not enormously robust and had yellowed with age."

JAMIE: "And the reason for that was that they were much cheaper. They did the job, just barely."

THE PLAN: The MythBusters' plan was to build and fly the lawn chair balloon just as it was described in the myth, which meant they had to prove that they could make a controlled descent by shooting out a portion of the balloons with a pellet pistol.

After a series of unsuccessful Dumpster dives, Adam finally gave in and bought a brand-new lawn chair for his flight. Because the model used by Larry Walters had been discontinued, the MythBusters settled on a more current model of aluminum construction.

The team planned on inflating four separate clusters of balloons. Each cluster was originally going to be tethered to Adam, two from the shoulders and two from the waist, while he sat in the lawn chair.

ADAM: "This foolish stunt was made even more foolish by doing it in a lawn chair. The original design of the balloon harness attached to the 'pilot's' body proved extremely uncomfortable. Also, the chair was way too flimsy and dangerous for an airborne flight."

The MythBusters eliminated the harness by attaching the balloons directly to a custom-made, steel-tubing-reinforced part lashed onto the seat of the lawn chair. This made the ride safer and much more comfortable.

After that, the MythBusters went balloon shopping. They eventually settled on cut-rate weather balloons. According to a balloon expert, the shelf life of weather balloons varies: Some are rated at one year, some at two years, while others might be rated up to five or six years. Larry Walters got his balloons from a surplus store that sold cheap latex balloons, which had a limited shelf life. Adam, in an effort to remain authentic to the original myth, selected cheap twenty-year-old balloons.

Adam's initial order of cylinders of helium gas provided only enough helium to fill a couple of weather balloons. Eventually, about twenty helium cylinders—or four times Adam's original estimate—were needed to fill all forty-two balloons.

ADAM: "The amount of helium needed to inflate forty-two balloons was enormous. The volume of helium was to be about thirty-three cubic feet. But because the helium was under pressure, even more was needed per balloon."

In theory, Adam was ready to leave the ground. But how would he be able to safely come back down?

THE EXPERIMENT: By five A.M. the next day, Adam was ready to recreate the mythical July 2, 1982, flight of Larry Walters in San Pedro.

ADAM: "The MythBusters utilized a staff of about fifteen people. In his original balloon voyage, Larry also had a lot of help. His main supporter was his girlfriend, Carol; she not only spent her life savings and maxed out her credit cards, she helped inflate the balloons."

Adam donned an orange jumpsuit so that he would be visible from a distance. After inflation, a couple of the cheap surplus balloons had already begun to disintegrate. (The balloons were much thinner than the MythBusters had originally thought.) By the time the lawn chair balloon was ready for launch, three of the twenty-year-old balloons had already expired. Time was running out.

Once a few of the water bottle sandbags that weighed down the chair were removed, Adam began his amazing ascent. In Larry's flight, there was enough pressure, force, and power stored in the balloons to shoot him upward at 1,000 feet per minute. Reportedly, two airline pilots spotted Larry's chair at about 16,000 feet. Adam's voyage was more controlled, and far safer: limited by the FAA and tied by lines to only 100 feet.

ADAM: "One of the things I had done for a living prior to *MythBusters* was flying people around as a stage rigger, so I had a lot of experience thinking through the safety of moving around live weight, especially mine. When we first talked about this myth, we talked about doing it on a tether or over water. Then, thinking it through from a rigging perspective, I realized that with so many balloons, more than half of those balloons would have to fail before anything catastrophic would happen. Since it was such a distributed load, all we needed was a tether to make sure I wasn't going to float up too high. In the end, I wish I had floated up a couple of hundred feet higher."

JAMIE: "According to the myth, a helicopter rescued Larry, but in reality, Larry dangerously crash-landed, blacking out a portion of Long Beach, California. When his lawn chair hit power lines, the only way to rescue him was to shut off an entire neighborhood's power supply. Adam's ride down was far smoother and better planned. The pellet pistol he used to shoot out the first few balloons effectively brought him back safely to earth in minutes."

ADAM: "I'd say we were one hundred percent successful. I got to about seventy-five feet, had a really great view, and the shooting of the balloons worked out really great."

MYTH STATUS: PLAUSIBLE

JAMIE: "Larry definitely could have done it. But it's a lot of work logistically. It takes a lot of time and helium to fill forty weather balloons."

The Federal Aviation Administration, though declining to be interviewed for the show, faxed in a document that confirmed many of the key details of Larry's flight, including his stiff $1,500 fine. Adjusted for inflation, a fine today would be even heftier.

ADAM: "I didn't have as much buoyancy as Larry Walters did. He had about four hundred pounds of buoyancy. We had about twenty pounds more than I weighed. Still, I could have easily gone over a couple of thousand feet, only a lot slower than he went."

PETER: "Plus, you would have touched down near the airport."

IMPORTANT SAFETY NOTE

☠ Under no circumstances should anyone try this at home. Not only is it logistically difficult—and extremely dangerous—to fly and land a lawn chair balloon, the FAA will arrest and fine anyone foolhardy enough to repeat lawn chair aviation history.

Could you survive falling 200 feet into water by throwing a hammer in first?

The Hammer Bridge Drop

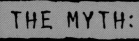**THE MYTH:** There's a modern myth circulating around the construction trade that if you fall off a high structure like a bridge or a crane over water and throw a hammer in front of you, it will save your life because the hammer will break the surface tension of the water.

THE PLAN: The plan was to drop Buster, the crash test dummy, into a body of water from some serious heights. The MythBusters conducted the experiment at Mare Island, a shipyard complex just north of San Francisco, using a huge crane capable of turning through 360 degrees. At its full extension, it reached up to around 150 feet, an ideal height to drop the hapless Buster off a pier and into the water.

Busting the hammer jump myth involved g-forces, terminal velocity, and surface tension.

ADAM: "This myth is based on the idea that if you fall from a really large height, hitting water is pretty much like hitting concrete. It doesn't move out of the way like we expect it to. It resists impact at that speed."

JAMIE: "By throwing a weight ahead of you, you're going to break the surface tension or possibly simply aerate the water to where it slows your deceleration."

ADAM: "The simple fact is, when Buster hits the water, the margin between life and death is going to be very small. It's only a tiny fraction of a second, and I suppose this hammer thing *could* make that difference. The stop is where you incur all that g-force on maximum impact."

In order to come up with consistent results, Jamie needed to create a rigging system from the very top of the crane so that

HISTORICAL NOTE

According to Stephen Cassady, author of *Spanning the Gate*, the hammer myth may have originated during construction of the Golden Gate Bridge. In 1937 twelve men fell 220 feet into the San Francisco Bay when a bridge section crashed into their safety net. Only one survived. Did his hammer break the fall?

PETER: "The tool belts these guys used had, among other things, spanners and hammers, so they might have a hundred pounds of tools around a tool belt. In consideration of the myth, I would think it would be reassuring to believe that if you're working high steel and you misstep, it would be nice if your tool belt went down first, broke the fall, and you survived."

every time Buster dropped, his fall would be consistent. Jamie suspended Buster and the hammer on a cable hundreds of feet above the water. Since he'd fall over a hundred feet several times, the dummy was rigged on a slide mechanism. To predict exactly where Buster and the hammer would hit the water, Jamie also adapted a quick-release cable and guide wires for the descent.

PETER: "Critical science testing like the Hammer Jump experiment requires calculating the force at impact, so Adam fit Buster with an accelerometer, the same type of device used by courier companies to see if your packages are being treated gently. It measures the energy generated by sudden stops. Placed inside the cranium of the dummy, the accelerometer measured the g-force when Buster hit the water. Being a regular crash test dummy, Buster's cavities were designed to hold smaller instruments for auto industry research, so Adam had to make extra room inside the dummy's head to accommodate the larger accelerometer."

Before dropping the dummy from the towering heights at Mare Island, the MythBusters tested the accelerometer with shorter rooftop drops. The meter was a go. After reinforcing Buster's arms and legs, it was time for the really big drops.

PETER: "This was the experiment where I found out that Jamie had a fear of heights. Jamie and I were up there for four or five hours. I was surprised, knowing how mentally strong Jamie is."

THE EXPERIMENT: With the dummy's accelerometer fully functional, it was time for Buster's high dives. The massive crane was rolled into position and raised to a soaring 150 feet. It was Jamie's task, unfortunately, to reach out and hook up the dummy to the quick-release. Because he was up so high, Jamie felt a stomach-churning combination of sheer terror and delight when he looked down at the water.

The guide wire kept the dummy on target as a high-speed camera recorded each moment of impact. The first drop was a back flop, not a belly flop. Buster experienced the full g-force that was possible and lost his left leg on the first drop. His other leg separated on the next drop.

ADAM: "It became pretty obvious that from that height you were completely screwed."

Because of Buster's missing legs, Adam and Jamie decided to start again in order to gather consistent data. They performed three subsequent control drops without legs and without a hammer.

ADAM: "Buster plummeted an average of sixty miles per hour with each plunge. Without the hammer, the accelerometer registered a g-force of two hundred eighty-seven, a devastating impact considering that an average car crash rates at around seventy g's."

It was time to attach the hammer. Would it break the surface tension and prove the myth? Even when the hammer fell first, the dummy still registered a shattering impact of 239 g's. The g-force was so great it yanked the skin coating from the dummy and rendered little floating scraps all over the site.

ADAM: "I don't think that losing Buster's legs affected our results. We got three good control drops without the hammer and three drops with the hammer. That's a reasonable data set to make an assessment as to whether or not the hammer helped."

THE RESULT: **JAMIE:** "My gut feeling is that the hammer probably had somewhat of an effect on the impact that the dummy received, but I don't think it was all that much. I don't think it would save your life. Jumping off hitting that water at a hundred and fifty feet would literally rip the limbs off your body."

Adam and Jamie compared the different impact curves downloaded from the accelerometer. With the hammer, the MythBusters recorded the g-force of two drops at 270 and 269 g's. Without the hammer, the plummets measured the g-force at 296 and 199 g's.

ADAM: "There's effectively no difference in the length of each curve. Each one is still between two hundred and three hundred g's. Even if the hammer helped a little bit, when Buster hit the water, he was going sixty-plus miles an hour, twice the speed that they test auto crashes."

WITH HAMMER G-FORCE = 270

NO HAMMER G-FORCE = 296

BUSTED

ADAM: "That a hammer breaks surface tension has no bearing in scientific fact or the application of the concept of the surface tension of the water. It might aerate the water, and if a sufficiently large object fell in front of you, like a Volkswagen, perhaps the bubbles created would aerate the water enough to slow down your deceleration to help you survive, but a hammer is not going to save you. The bottom line is our data doesn't show any real effect of the hammer at all."

JAMIE: "I would say that this myth is busted."

SCIENTIFIC PRINCIPLE

ADAM: "This experiment involved collision physics and human biodynamics. The amount of g's Buster took hitting the water was really shocking. When you're in a car accident, you might take seventy or eighty g's, but falling a hundred fifty feet, Buster was taking something like three hundred g's."

The MythBusters thank:

THE ELEVATOR OF DEATH: Lester Appel

BURIED ALIVE!: Heather Joseph-Witham, Brother Guire Cleary, Kellie L. Gillespie, Dr. William Miller

POPPY SEED DRUG TEST: Heather Joseph-Witham, Larry Dougherty, Dr. Kent Holtorf (author of *Ur-In Trouble*)

DOWN WITH THE *MYTHTANIC!*: Heather Joseph-Witham, Greg Urban, Sean Wheelef

THE MIDAS MYTH OF GOLDFINGER: Shirley Eaton, Dr. Ronald R. Brancaccio, Dr. Remo Morelli

JET-ASSISTED CHEVY OR JATO CAR: Andy Granatelli, Bob Stein, Eric and Dirk Gates

THE SCUBA DIVER FOREST FIRE MYTH: Heather Joseph-Witham, Officers Odersom and Hopkins, Craig Jacobsen, Jay Meiswinkel, Sal Zammitti

PING-PONG SALVAGE: Scott Pryor, Robert Flores, Rachel Saunders

MICROWAVE MADNESS: Heather Joseph-Witham, Rick Mattoon, Michael Friedman

NEEDLE IN THE HAYSTACK: Mike Barrett, Cathe A. Ray

KILLER QUICKSAND: Gerald Gray, Thomas Holzer

THE ROWING WATER SKIER: The Stanford University Varsity Rowing Team, Craig Amerkhanian, Willi Ellermeier, Jon Albin, Heather Joseph-Witham

EXPLODING IMPLANTS!: Heather Joseph-Witham, Dr. Gregory Georgiade, Dr. Richard Vann

MYTHBUSTERS CAR CAPERS: Cadillac, Ben Rillie

CHICKEN GUN: Heather Joseph-Witham, Mike Ebert, Anthony Tarantino, Bruce Bradford

YOU CAN'T BEAT THE BREATH TEST!: San Francisco Police Department Crime Lab, Officer Bruce Gadroon, Heather Joseph-Witham

THE GREAT CEMENT TRUCK MIX-UP: Ron Nunez, Jack Morocco, Frank Doyle

MYTHBUSTERS COLA MYTHS: Dr. Paul Turek

IN SEARCH OF THE BROWN NOTE: John Meyer, Roger Schwenke, Paul Mahar

EXPLODING CDS?: David Bunzel, Kyman Jeung

LARRY'S LAWN CHAIR BALLOON: Lakshmi Bhukta, Mark Barry